The Grandfield Servants

Song of Destiny

* * *

Olwyn Harris

ISBN   Softcover   978-1-923021-40-2

           eBook   978-1-923021-41-9

Unless otherwise stated Scriptures quoted here are from the King James Version (Authorised version). First published in 1611. Quoted from the KJV Classic Reference Bible, copyright 1983 by the Zondervan Corporation.

The hymn –"In the Garden", 1912 by C Austin Miles – copyright – public domain.

Published by: Reading Stones Publishing

Helen Brown & Wendy Wood

Woodwendy1982.wixsite.com/readingstones

Cover Design: Olwyn Harris. Some of the cover elements were created using AI Technology. The image of the house, 'But-Har-Gra' was obtained from Wikipedia.org and used under the following licences. Permission is granted to copy, distribute and/or modify this document under the terms of the GNU Free Documentation License, Version 1.2 or any later version published by the Free Software Foundation; with no Invariant Sections, no Front-Cover Texts, and no Back-Cover Texts. A copy of the license is included in the section entitled *GNU Free Documentation License*. And was modified by Olwyn Harris.

For more copies contact the publisher at:

Glenburnie

212 Glenburnie Road

ROB ROY NSW 2360

Mobile: 0422 577 663

Email: Readingstonespublishing@gmail.com

Authors Note

When I was twelve my parents were gifted with a holiday at 'But-Har-Gra' in Sydney. Staying in such an imposing manor-house captured the imagination of this country girl. I was fascinated by the tiled mosaics on the verandah; the grand sweeping polished timber staircase; the thick, wide internal walls that naturally insulated the rooms, so they were cool in summer; the grass tennis courts and the majestic Camphor Laurel trees in the garden. I also remember being told the house had been seconded by the government during WWI and was converted to a war-hospital for injured soldiers, and it became an orphanage in the second world war. The stories of this series are set in a similar house with a similar history. They fulfil a childhood wondering of who might have inhabited such a place, and what might have become of the servants who worked there.

~ Olwyn

Dedication:

For Mum... who taught me to sing the song in my heart
because the music is there, not just to make a point.

Part 1

The Prelude of Grandfield

1909

Miss Lambert rapped her baton on the music stand. "Come now my Little Lambs, we are going to do our warm-up game. Remember we don't do 'exercises'... because that doesn't sound much like fun. We do intentional games. Everyone in a circle. Now who is going to start?" She scanned the group and focussed on a girl with pigtails and spectacles who was older than the others. "Ellie, you can start as we take a nice slow cold drink before we walk around the zoo, visiting all our marvellous choir animals."

She passed the baton to Ellie who waved it high, "Hmm–Hmm–Ahhh!" and she dropped her arms.

"That's right! Beautifully done. Each of you share a long deep drink with Ellie to start our excursion around the zoo. Everyone together! Hmm–Hmm–Ahhh!"

Each child followed Ellie's lead, arms flaying enthusiastically, as they repeated the exercise three or four times and then Miss Lambert flipped over the picture of a glass of water on her pinboard that stood in the middle of a myriad of animals. Ellie passed the baton to Flip.

Flip looked a little panicked, but Ellie leant in and quietly whispered, "Snake..." He nodded and took the baton and wove it about in the air. "Sss – Sss – Sss." His actions were copied by all the other children. "Sss – Sss – Sss." Miss Lambert flipped over the snake picture on her board.

Flip passed the baton to Jimmy, who started preening like a cat. "Mee – Mou – Marr". The cat picture was turned over. The baton went around the group until all the pictures on Miss Lamberts board disappeared – bees buzzing; donkeys braying; whales sighing; lions growling; rabbits humming; cows lowing... until the baton finally was passed to Anna. She had refused the baton to this point, so that she could be the lamb. The lamb was the last and most prestigious animal because it marked the close of the game. "Baa – Blah – Baa – Blah," she bleated, luring the group away as wandering sheep. Miss Lambert took a stuffed woollen bone and passed it to Flip, whose job was now to round up all the bleating sheep. When the sheepdog touched a sheep with the bone, they would join him as a dog, panting and huffing with "Bow – Wowing," until all the sheep were either back in the circle of chairs that was their pen... or they had been transformed into panting sheepdogs.

Miss Lambert smiled and clapped enthusiastically. "Well done my Little Lambs! Well done! Miss Lambert is proud of her little flock! Today we are going to start putting together the parts to the new song we have been practicing." She went over to the piano and instructed the children to gather around. She played a cord. "Okey-dokey, my Little Lambs, let's start. Remember we have snacks after this." Slowly she paced them through their parts, practicing their harmonies, until they were... perhaps not singing like the melodies of morning magpies... but definitely enthusiastic lambs.

* * *

After the choir practice, Anna stood on the steps of the church hall. She had begged her mother to follow Miss Lambert's advice in allowing her to join the community choir. Mother had finally relented, and now Anna stood watching the group demolish biscuits, hot buns and sausage rolls laid out on the table. Anna wondered how, when they lived on exactly the same street, how the food offered here at this address would generate this feeding frenzy, whereas the high teas hosted on the lawn of Grandfield Park were so dignified. This was a rowdy and unruly affair, and it was not at all what Anna was used to. It lacked taste and decorum – that is what her mother would say. Miss Lambert came and stood with her as the others were leaving the hall. "Are you feeling poorly Anna?" she asked quietly.

"Oh no, Miss Lambert. Tibby will be picking me up very soon. I will just wait here, until he comes."

"Anna, I know you are new to the group, and I know this is very different to the private lessons we have at home. But it is my hope that these afternoons will be pleasant for you. Being with other children should be fun. Did you enjoy the practice today?" In Miss Lambert's mind, the privilege of living in that big old-fashioned house, with old-fashioned servants, and old-fashioned views about girls, was fraught with danger; danger that Anna would grow up isolated. Isolated from companionship of children her own age, with similar interests. It wasn't just her social wellbeing that prompted Miss Lambert's insistence that Anna be here. It effected Anna musically as well. There was no doubt she was gifted, yet without this, she would never experience singing in harmony with other voices or performing together in a beautiful melodic blend.

Anna tilted her head and sighed. She was comfortable with her solo life, where she was the leading lady. "I don't know anyone here. What if they don't like me? How would I enjoy it then?"

"But that is just it. This is a chance for you to get to know them. But you need to start by talking with the others. Standing in the corner is not getting to know them."

"I much prefer having you all to myself. That way I can ask you my questions without other people thinking I'm stupid."

"No one thinks you are stupid," Miss Lambert said fervently.

Anna was about to reply when Tibby drove up in the phaeton. Saved by the old-fashioned steward and his old-fashioned horse and buggy. Anna didn't mind at all. She liked Tibby.

* * *

2

"Oh. Reverend, you came." Mrs Pollard stood at the door with a frown. Her drawn face looked as crinkled and as tattered as her dress.

Reverend Peters adjusted his hat. "I'm sorry, perhaps you did not want me to come? I had received a message, but if there was some mistake..." Football was Reverend Peters' one vice, and he left the game before it was finished to come here. There was no way he would be able to catch the end of the game now, so he might as well continue with this pastoral visit even if it was unbidden and unwanted.

"Oh, no – I didn't mean nothing by it, Reverend. I did send a message... it's just I never did expect you would actually come." She stepped back wringing her hands. "Come in."

He walked through the door. Three sets of eyes blinked out from the shadows under the table. Reverend Peters gently couched down and locked eyes with the oldest urchin. "I was wondering if your brother and sister would be interested in some fat, juicy mulberries? I have brought some for you all."

They looked at him sceptically, but when the minister passed each child a stained handmade paper cone containing fresh plump berries, they grinned and nodded. The oldest noticed with some pride, that he had been designated as the keeper of their special treat. The kids stayed under the table and eagerly ate their berries.

Reverend Peters had bought the berries from Miss Anna Whitaker as he had walked past Grandfield Park gates. She had set up an enterprising street stall, and was selling berries, waiting for the crowd from the football game to come past. Grandfield Park was a big grand old house, with a gate that was equally big and grand. That mansion was a vestige of the past: the matriarchal estate that was built when their suburb was newly settled and acquiring land parcels was often associated with nepotism and guarantees of political support. Even though Australia was no longer a young colony of the British Empire, Mr and Mrs Whitaker still held onto those grand feudal ideals; frustrated by the reality that they were surrounded by ordinary people in ordinary houses, rather than the prestige of the social strata they identified with.

Reverend Peters wanted to encourage Anna. She was delighted Anna was inclined to join their community choir at the church hall, run by Miss Lambert. He liked the girl and hoped that participating in the choir, would foster ordinary healthy friendships and that alone, would do Anna good.

Reverend Peters stood up. "I brought a cup of berries for Ellie as well. She is our choir's nightingale after all." He looked around. "Where is she?"

* * *

"Hey Ellie..." Billy said with a bashful grin as he poked his head around the fence by the water tank.

"Billy! What are you doing here?" Ellie balanced the bucket and turned on the tap.

"I came here to see ya."

"Oh..." She looked around again and no one else was about. That was unusual. Billy usually had a group of hangers-on. It was as natural as breathing for him. People followed Billy around. People listened to what he said. People copied what he did. 'People' mostly being a rag-tag number of bored young kids with nothing better to do.

Billy nodded confidently. "You know that story... that one about Robin Hood. That gave me an idea. I'm gunna do that. Yep. That's me. I've already started doing that... me and my boys."

"You've started what?" Ellie looked startled. "Billy what have you done?"

"Well, The Hood flogs from the rich to give to the poor." So, he told her his plan, beginning with the street-stall outside *that big Grandfield House... on Silverspoon Lane... selling mulberries that only grows on trees that the birds eat for free anyways*". Billy leaned against the water tank and squared his shoulders. "But it didn't really work out this time," he confessed. "But I'm not giving up. I'm going back after the game to finish it..."

Ellie stared at him horrified and shook her head. "Billy, you are not Robin Hood."

"Course not... I don't like green. But I am *like* him in other ways. Billy the Hood. I got me a band of men, and we don't like them Silverspoons neither. 'Cause they've got plenty and that's not fair. And you be like that Marion maid."

"Oh, give me a break Billy. This is serious. If you go around stealing, you will get in trouble. You've got to stop this."

"It's not really stealing. Not when they deserve it to be taken and we don't have nothing. Besides, when did you become such a prude? I only did it for you."

"You did it because you think it is cool that those kids do whatever you say. You have to stop!"

"You can't make me! But I can make *you* change your mind. I *will* change your mind. You will... when I give you money for your kid sister so your Mum can get a doctor, you will see that I'm right..."

Ellie stared at him with fire in her eyes. "Not all things can be solved by throwing money at them Billy. Now, go!" she hissed under her breath. "I have to go back inside."

"Ellie!" Her mum's voice came from the living room, strained and scratchy. "Are you on the roof again? Ellie! Come down! I need your help!"

Ellie sighed. Her mother was right. Her ideas and ambitions were climbing too high. And it was time to come back down to earth. Her Mum needed her.

Billy pulled at her arm as she turned away. "I won't give up Ellie. I won't. I will get money to buy you pretty girl-things, and then you will know that I did right by you. And then you will agree that you are my girl."

Ellie shook him free and rolled her eyes. "I gotta go." She turned quickly and jumped up the back stairs, missing the second wobbly step. Generally, she liked Billy, but this was going too far. She didn't want to be his 'girl'. Trying to keep him out of trouble all the time was draining. She had enough going on looking after her brothers and sister. Ellie was nearly thirteen. Most girls her age had a job, but she needed to stay home and help look after her family because Mum had her hands full with their new baby sister. Billy was right about one thing though... the money would help. But it would take more help than the takings from a kid's street-stall to fix a little baby who was so sick she turned grey.

* * *

Ellie walked inside and her mother was sitting on the saggy lounge beside the Reverend, rocking the baby restlessly. She was telling him what the midwife had said, and what the doctor had said. That there was nothing that they could do. Her mother's voice was quiet and serious. "So, Mister, I am looking for a miracle. I'm wanting you to ask God to do His thing, so my baby will live. I'll do anything. We will even come back to church, more than just singing practice, and we will clean up real nice. I just want my Myrtle to be okay. If only you could just see her like I do... when she ain't this ashy grey colour...". Her voice trailed off in despair. And Reverend Peters quietly talked to her. Ellie couldn't really hear what he said. Perhaps it was about what her mother needed to do to get God on side. What she did hear was Mum's inconsolable sobbing.

Ellie bundled her brothers and sister over to the basin to wash the berry juice off their fingers and rinsed out a stale threadbare washer and scrubbed their mulberry stained cheeks. "Looks like you got more berries on the outside, than the inside."

"Reverend Peters made us save some for you Ellie," said her brother.

Ellie knelt down and smiled at him. "Did he now? Well, that is real kind of you. Bet it was hard not to just eat them. How about I share them with you and the others? Let's make this treat go the distance for all of us." That was something Miss Lambert did at the Church Hall every choir day. She miraculously made the afternoon tea after practice go the distance for the whole group. Miss Lambert called it 'Feeding the five thousand'. Ellie smiled sadly and looked at her brothers with affection. "That's something special now, isn't it? Where's Hazel?"

"Over there with Mummy... and baby Myrtle..."

Ellie looked over at the group huddled on the lounge cradling their baby sister. Hazel hovered over her mother's shoulder, her little round face awash with tears. Her mother had shrunken back into the grubby blanket thrown over the lounge to hide the rips in the faded upholstery.

Reverend Peters sat there, pale and sombre, silently mourning the calamity visiting this family. The arrival of a baby was supposed to be full of joy and tired nights and lusty cries. Even he could tell that Baby Myrtle would not be part of this family much longer, and he wasn't even a medical man.

* * *

3

"Hi Anna..." Ellie came and stood by Anna. "It is nice having another girl who can sing harmonies in the choir. You have a nice voice."

It was not often that Anna didn't have something to say, but it was also true that Anna was rarely placed in unfamiliar territory where she was obliged to function outside her comforts. "Thanks," Anna said tentatively. "And my name is Anna*belle*". She didn't want to get too friendly with this girl. That would be disloyal to Chrissy. Chrissy was her best friend. Anna looked down the road. Tibbs was never late, but perhaps he was today because Chrissy was sick. Chrissy was Tibby's daughter. It was important that Anna get home. She had to. Anna tried to avoid the practice this afternoon, but today of all days, her mother insisted. Anna felt like she was abandoning her friend. More than a friend... soul-sister... more like blood-sister. Sure, Chrissy might be the daughter of the household staff at Grandfield, but to Anna, Chrissy was everything. No one understood that. Even talking with this new girl, felt like a betrayal to every pact, game, secret, chore, mission, joke and laughter Anna had shared with Chrissy.

Ellie cleared her throat and tried again. "I like your clothes, Annabelle. You have some very pretty dresses. I like that your hats always match." Miss Lambert had encouraged Ellie to try and be friendly. She even suggested complimenting her clothes. It was a stupid mission. What would she, Ellie Pollard, ever have in common with someone like Annabelle Whitaker who lived in a flash old house like Grandfield?

Anna looked at Ellie and felt disgusted that they were talking about wardrobe. Pretty dresses and matching hats were the least important thing in the entire world. She actually thought Ellie would be the type of girl who would be interested in more significant things than clothes and appearances. It was weird that the plain girl with plaits and glasses sounded very 'Grandfield'. Dresses didn't matter. Not really. Anna pressed her mouth and then tilted her head to look down the road for Tibby. "You know. I think I am going to walk home."

"Really? You never walk home. Tibby always picks you up."

Anna looked at Ellie quickly. "How do you know Tibby? He belongs to us."

"Everyone knows Mister Tiberius Barnes... he is one of the elders at our church. And he teaches Sunday School. And he is not *yours* at all. He is everyone's friend."

"I knew him first."

"Well, I've known him longer," Ellie said.

"That's not true. I've known him my entire life!"

"Me too. And since I'm older than you... that means what I said is true."

Anna frowned. "Humph! I wonder why Chrissy has never joined your stupid choir. If Tibby is so tight with you and your church, she would have come."

"She tried out, but she can't sing. Even Miss Lambert couldn't get her to stay in tune. She used to help with chairs and the chores, but she doesn't do that anymore. That's when Flip took over that."

Anna stared at Ellie in mortification. That was the most vile thing anyone could say in the entire world. Chrissy could do anything! And it didn't even matter if she wasn't perfect at it. Anna, if nothing else, was a very loyal friend. She straightened her back. "I'm walking home. Good day!" And she tilted her chin, adjusted her hat and her jacket, stepped onto the path, and turned down the street.

It wasn't far, but it was a walk that Anna had never done by herself before. Chrissy was sick... and if that meant she needed to climb high mountains to prove Chrissy meant the world to her, she would do it. Ellie might not have pretty clothes, but she was as stuck up as the rest of Grandfield Park.

It seemed that no one understood how horrible it was that Chrissy was so badly sick. Anna had never felt so abandoned. But as she walked down that street alone, the only sound that she noticed was the magpies singing on the rooftops, and Anna found a new idea. She would sing a song for Chrissy. Perhaps that might make her feel better. Even Ellie said she had a nice voice... and Ellie was the one everyone talked about when it came to music. Suddenly a magpie swooped down, and Anna ducked as her beak clacked near her ear. Anna squealed and screamed and ran for the gates of Grandfield. Her mother was right; it was dangerous outside her Grandfield world.

Ellie watched Anna walk away and shook her head. She could not believe how snobby some people were. Just because they have a nice singing voice, and live in a nice house, and wear nice clothes, that didn't make them nice people. Then Ellie shrugged and turned to go home. Well, she had done what Miss Lambert had asked her to do. She couldn't make *Annabelle* be her friend. And she didn't need a snobby person as her friend anyway.

The disappointing thing was that Miss Lambert did not understand that Ellie had tried. Miss Lambert had been pretty severe on the whole group when she found out about Anna's decision not to come back to the community choir. There was a whole speech about the ethics of community, and that a choir was not just about singing together, but about giving everyone a chance to have a voice, which started by being kind to each other. Ellie couldn't understand why so many people insisted on advocating for Anna when she had every advantage. The choir didn't need her... or her parent's money.

* * *

4

"Hey! Look who it is. It is flippin' Flip! Wanna know what he reminds me of... one of them fishes, flippin' around on the wharf when them old codgers are fishin'. Flip. Flip. Flippin'. Flip! Flip!" Flip closed his ears against their taunts. Perhaps today he would escape. He just wanted to get to choir practice. Flip set his jaw and kept walking. This was the hardest thing about being part of the Community Choir. Getting there meant walking past the spare block where the young kids who hung around Billy had built a kind of club house out of old tea chests, and boxes salvaged from the alley behind the fruit and vege market. Billy kept telling the story of Robin Hood and lapped up their adoring devotion with the air of a hero. Flip likened it to a mangy dog drinking from the water-troughs placed along the road for the horses. Even calling their construction on the spare block a 'clubhouse' was sanitising what was really a pack of rogue strays living in a dump.

Flip was pretty sure that not all the boys wanted to be part of Billy's take on Robin Hood's band of merry men, but it was easier to go along with it than subjecting themselves to the constant barrage of harassment that would come their way if they didn't submit to 'club-rules'. Flip was familiar with their harassment. To him it was the price of staying out a trouble for his Mum's sake. She said she was so proud of him, and he wasn't going to do anything that would disappoint her faith in him. Flip just kept his head down and increased his pace walking towards the Community Hall.

"Hey Flip, wait up!"

Flip jolted and turned around to see Ellie running towards him, her borrowed music books bouncing under her arm. He blushed and slowed his walking just a bit. He liked Ellie. She was kind and pretty and her voice was like velvet. He'd heard people say that Ellie Pollard would make their community famous one day with her singing. Her voice was that good.

He'd had a secret crush on Ellie since the very first time he had heard her sing. It was a secret because Billy told everyone that Ellie was "his girl". But Flip could tell that they were not really 'together'; he never saw any evidence that they were actually friends. She was a trophy that Billy hung around his neck like the pig's tooth that he stole from some old man. What a miserable victory that was, yet Billy saw it as an epic conquest. He wanted that tooth. He got it. That was his style – flaunting his bragging rights over any possession. Ellie was the same.

As soon as Ellie changed her pace to walk with Flip, he was uncomfortable. Without moving his head, he glanced across at her. "What are you doing?"

"I thought I would like to walk with you."

"Why?"

"You are different Flip... different to the others."

"Different how?"

"Different in that you don't care what Billy thinks."

"Maybe you don't either, because if he sees you walking with me, that'll mean trouble."

"We're just going to the same place. Don't you want me to walk with you?"

"Nah. I like it. I just don't think Billy will like it. He says you are his girl."

"Of course he does. Doesn't mean he ever actually asked me, or that I actually am. I am my own person," she said with a tilt of her chin.

"Maybe. Maybe not."

"I am! I can prove it!" And she leant over and kissed him on the cheek.

"Ellie... I...". Whatever Flip was going to say was cut short by the whoop of eight lads running at them in a rush. They pushed Ellie out of the way and tackled Flip to the ground, knocking him flying. He landed hard under the crush of their bodies, and they started beating up on him. Billy sauntered up in the rear and surveyed their flaying arms.

Ellie screamed, "Billy! Stop them!"

"Now why would I? He was talking with my girl."

"We were just walking together. Stop them!"

"He needs to know that no one walks, or talks, with *my* girl."

"I am not your property Billy! I can have friends."

"Sure, you can. But only if I say you can, and with whoever I say. Now tell me you won't have anything to do with this twerp ever again, and I'll call off the dogs." He turned to the frenzied crush and called out "More!" The energy, noise and turmoil went up a notch.

"I won't talk with him Billy, I won't. Just stop it!" Ellie's lip trembled; tears streamed down her face. Flip was right. She didn't have the autonomy she thought she did. "I'll do whatever you want. Just tell them to stop."

"Now tell him you're my girl. It's that simple."

"Okay. I'll do it. Call them off..."

Billy stuck his grubby fingers in his mouth, and let out an ear-piercing whistle, and the boys fell back dusting off their hands on their britches. "Okay. Now say it."

"Now?"

"Yes now." He raised his arm like a racing umpire, ready to give the signal for them to start again.

"No. No. Wait. I'll say it." She went over to where Flip was crumpled in a heap. "You were right," she whispered quietly through her tears as she crouched beside him. "I'm so sorry Flip. Please forgive me..." She stood up and swallowed hard as she cleared her throat. "Flip Sinclair, you need to do know that Billy Stamford is my boyfriend," she said, and her voice shuddered as she took a deep breath.

"Say it louder!" he said.

"I'm going out with Billy now."

"Sweet!" Billy dropped his hand fast, and the boys rushed in. They pulled Flip to his feet and bundled him across the street and dunked him in a water trough used to water horses. Then they disappeared like cockroaches into the cracks in the pavement. Flip raised his drenched head to see Billy pull a sparkly broach from his pocket and pin it on her blouse. Then he grabbed Ellie's arm and marched her down the road towards the community hall.

* * *

Next week Flip turned up at the community hall as usual and arranged the chairs just the way Miss Lambert liked them. Ellie arrived before the others and went over to Flip, quietly helping him. He noticed that she wasn't wearing Billy's broach today. He nervously looked around to see who was tailing her to report back to Billy. Little Jimmy wasn't here yet. Flip wondered if he was Billy's eyes. Probably.

"It is good to see you today, Flip," Ellie said quietly. "Choir is the only break I get from the chores at home, so I try to get here early."

He shrugged and smiled. He liked it that they had this time together. Alone. "My Mum is keen that I still do this; the Doc seems to think it will help. I dunno about that, but it is enough that Mum at least thinks so. Otherwise, I probably wouldn't bother. Getting here is a little rough."

"What did she say when you got beat up?"

"Not much to start with. She was pretty mad. Later she said there are two types of 'strong'. One is the Billy sort, the type that is

26

mean and unfair. The other might not look tougher, but it looks out for those that we love. She told me I need to choose which sort of 'Strong' I want to be known for." He shrugged. "I thought about that. I don't like Billy and his sort, so not going for that."

"How come they let you through today?" asked Ellie quickly. The bruising across his eye was dark and turning slightly yellow around the edges. His arms and legs were still purple and blotchy, but there were no fresh cuts.

"They didn't. I went the long way. Took three times as long... but I figured that if I know where the mulga snake lives, no point poking my hand down the log."

Ellie giggled. Flip was funny. And then sobered. "I'm sorry about what I said Flip. I really am. I only said it 'cause I was scared of what they were doing." Ellie was quiet that day. She sang of course, but her thoughts were consumed by Flip, battered and bruised on the outside, but so quiet and respectful and strong on the inside. Flip was right: he didn't look that tough, but she saw something different. She stayed back to help him pack up the chairs. "Guess I'm not as strong as you Flip. Wish I was. I don't like Billy's type of tough either."

"Don't worry about it, Ellie. I know that. Still, I reckon you've got all sorts of courage inside you."

"Me? Like what?"

"Like singing in front of people. That's really brave. I can barely talk if there are two people staring at me. And what about all the things you do for your Mum... looking after your brothers and sister and such, while little Myrtle is sick. That's gotta be tough. Sometimes I wish I had brothers and sisters instead of being an only child; other times I reckon it's just simpler... because I only have to look out for my Mum and me."

Ellie smiled sadly. She wished... oh how she wished that she had Flip's type of tough inside of her. "Thanks Flip. You are a good friend. I am so sorry."

"Ellie, just knowing that you are my friend means a lot. And I get that it needs to be a secret between us, because if Billy finds out, it won't be good for either of us... and I want you to be safe more than anything."

Ellie nodded and reached out and shook his hand. "Secret friends forever." And they twisted their hands in an awkward secret hold, sealing their pact. Not that she considered that being with Billy was any form of safe. It's just she didn't know what else she could do. Besides, perhaps this was a way she could protect Flip too. She ached for a day when she didn't have to push her true friendships down just because someone else thought it wasn't right.

* * *

Ellie's Mum had warned her. She said that unless God answered her prayers, little Myrtle would go to be an angel very soon. But it is one thing to be told something like that, and it is another thing to actually understand what that means, or to be prepared for such an event. Every night Ellie heard her Mum moving about, she would ease out of bed trying not to disturb her siblings, to check if she needed anything. But this night Ellie watched from the doorway. Her Mum was sitting on the lounge, rocking and rocking, back and forth. Ellie could see baby Myrtle was wrapped up too heavily and her mother was clinging too tightly. Mum wasn't saying anything, her eyes had a glazed grief-stricken sort of panic around them as she murmured little snippets that didn't make sense. Myrtle was silent. Ellie didn't do anything other than find a light wrap and put it around her Mum's shoulders, and then silently sat on the far side of the lounge for a long time. Slowly Ellie began to sing the gentle lullaby that she had heard her mum whisper to her sister when nothing would settle her restlessness or revive her limp muscle tone. Gradually, her Mum loosened her hold, swayed in time of the lilt of the music, tears streaming down her cheeks. Ellie softly sang it again and again. When the light of the new day started to bleach the darkness, Ellie changed out of her nightdress and noiselessly slipped out of the house, to fetch Reverend Peters.

It was one of those days that you don't forget. The kids were grave and silent, devoid of the pranks and squabbles that normally filled the house with noise. A few people from the neighboured filed through their shabby little living room. Some even brought flowers. That seemed strange to Ellie. The flowers in these bouquets were so pretty; it seemed a pity that something so tragic had to happen to have their beauty, colour and scent fill the house.

There was a brief service by the grave side. It was a distressing affair. For a little life, so short and unremarkable, Ellie could barely understand why it ripped so viciously at her heart. Her mother's face took on the same ashen colour that was Myrtle's complexion in life. Ellie had to coax her to even eat. Ellie wasn't sure, but she wondered if this meant her mother was afflicted with Myrtle's illness and it might not be long before her mother would also die. It was another worry layered on worry. Ellie determined that she would do whatever she could to look after her family until her Mum was well again.

Ellie's stepfather didn't feature in their life very much. He didn't even appear for the funeral. It seemed his pattern was that he would come home long enough to get her mother pregnant, and then he'd leave again. What he did while he was away, Ellie wasn't sure. Her mother said he was working, but she also saw the deep lines of worry around her Mum's eyes as she sat at the table with bills in her hands. Ellie could not understand that. It was not like they lived extravagant lives. When her Mum wasn't in the room, Ellie would look through those papers and try and make sense of them.

After Sunday Bible class one day, Tibby Barnes gently drew Ellie aside. "How are you going Ellie? I know you all miss your little Myrtle so much. How is your Mum?"

Ellie looked at him with wide eyes that seemed to be even larger behind the lenses of her reading glasses. The church had pulled the money together for her spectacles so she could read music. There was something about the compassionate tone in Tibby's voice that caused tears to pool in her eyelids. "Oh Mr Barnes, I don't know what we are going to do. Mum needs me at home, but I am nearly thirteen now... I should be able to get a job to help with the bills. I think that would help more than sweeping the porch. There is less to do now that Little Myrtle is gone, but Mum is... she is so sad, and she is not coping with the boys." She sighed. It seemed so wrong to say it like that.

"Are you looking for a job?" said Mr Barnes gently.

"Well, no... but only because I don't know what I could even do. And like I said, Mum needs me at home. Lots of people say there will be other babies, and time will heal, and that Myrtle is a little angel in a better place... but it doesn't seem to make a difference, so I need to stay close."

Tibby took her by the hand and gently led her to a chair, and he pulled up a stool beside her. He sat down at a respectful distance "Ellie it is hard when we lose someone we love. When we love all in, it doesn't matter whether we have loved for a few months, or a lifetime. You are very wise to allow your mother to grieve in her own way."

Ellie gasped. She had been so absorbed in her own worry that she had forgotten Mr Barnes had recently lost his own daughter. Chrissy passed not that long ago. Double pneumonia. It felt like having a companion in her pain. Someone who really understood her. "I'm so sorry Mr Barnes... I forgot about Chrissy."

"Oh Ellie, sometimes our world shrinks small, just so we can get through. I feel that too, you know. And it's okay. I know you were a good friend to her."

Ellie's tears spilt over. If only her stepfather was more like Mr Barnes. Nothing would seem so impossibly hard. Tibby handed her a kerchief, and she sniffed. "Thank you, Mr Barnes."

"Ellie, you can call me Tibby if you like. Most people do, and I am kind of used to it."

"Oh, I don't know Mr Barnes... maybe..."

Tibby continued. "I would like to suggest something to you Ellie. I know Marlie would appreciate some help in the kitchen, now that she doesn't have her best helper anymore." Tibby swallowed hard, and his voice cracked. He took a breath. "Chrissy used to do things like washing up and peeling vegetables. I wonder if you could come for a couple of hours each day and help my Marlie with those sorts of things. The pay won't be much, but it might help a bit. What do you think?"

"You will pay? You are offering me a job at Grandfield Park?"

"I am. Making sure everything runs smoothly at Grandfield is one of my responsibilities. If you are inclined, I think this is a way we can help each other. I know you work hard at home, and I am sure you would work hard for Marlie in the kitchen as well."

"Oh, I will! I will." Only a few of hours a day would mean that she could still be at home most of the time. Her Mum would hardly miss her. All those promises from Billy had come to nothing of course. He was just like her stepfather. Just like the wind: puffed out and blustering when he was around and then disappeared like a vapour and was gone. Anyway, she didn't want Billy's stolen trinkets boosting her family's pantry. That didn't seem right. Ellie held tightly to the idealism of Flip's sort of tough. The kind of strong that protects and looks out for your family by doing the better thing, regardless of what it looks like on the outside. Tibby had that same kind of tough... like Flip who stayed around to look after his Mum. It was his example which inspired her to hang in there and help. Even when it was hard, that was what loving all-in meant... like Tibby said.

* * *

33

Part 2

Melody of Pain

1915

6

It had been six years since Ellie started working in Grandfield's kitchen. Every day, weekends aside, Ellie would arrive just after breakfast, wash dishes, and then help Marlie prepare the meals for lunch and dinner. Marlie would offer her extra hours if Mrs Whitaker, the lady of the house, had a function planned and needed someone to serve. Or she would help Marlie in the kitchen with the extra preparation and cooking. This arrangement suited Ellie well enough. And then war broke out. Young men, and not-so-young men enlisted in droves. Faces disappeared from the neighbourhood. Billy was one. All the boys from the Community Choir signed up, except Flip. He tried many times, before he also finally wore a uniform. Women were equally patriotic, handing out leaflets to promote all sort of things in a drive to support their local heroes. Knitting pools sprang up in almost every lounge room. Care kits were enthusiastically assembled and dropped off at collection points. Rations were not an imposition, but just another way they could support 'the boys' overseas. Every back yard had a "Victory Garden", and the Church Hall cultivated their own community garden on every inch of their block and even installed a chook-run to help those who didn't have much.

* * *

Ellie climbed the tank-stand and swung over to the roof. It had been a long time since she came up here in the morning to watch the sunrise. It was quiet here, away from the noise of inside. She could hear her newest sister crying lustily, the outcome of her stepfather dropping in before he enlisted. Her brothers were already scrapping over some toy that had transformed into military weaponry for their game. Ellie stared at the clouds as they blushed pink over the neighbourhood rooftops. The stillness of the morning was punctuated by the chorus of sparrows, chirping and whistling their delight in this fresh new day. 'The Lord's mercies are new every morning', Ellie read in the bible Marlie had given her. She often forgot that each day starts the same... with sunrise and birdsong. No wonder she had spent so much time up here on the roof as a kid.

A little butcher bird alighted on the gutter nearby and he tilted his head as he looked at her with his bright little eye. Ellie wondered what that little black-and-white bird thought as he listened to the chorus of sparrows. Did he worry that his rendition of his morning song might be considered poorly by this audience?

Then he titled his head again and started singing. His gorgeous morning song had Ellie captivated. Her heart constricted in pure wonder as she listened with joy to his warbling melody. It was a sound that was purer than any aria Miss Lambert played on her gramophone. The little bird sang such a range of notes, with whistles and warbles; he kept going and going as if his little heart would burst

Ellie envied the devotion he showed to his art. He sang his composition in his own way, completely unconcerned that the backing vocals were only sparrows, or that their voices did not compare to his. Nor was he worried that the world was being torn apart by war. He didn't change his melody because Ellie might not appreciate it, or that she might admire another version more highly. He sang, free from decrees prescribing the range of the notes, or metering the tempo, or dictating the melody. He sang, not because he had an opinion to indoctrinate, or the war-cause to proselytise, or a point of view to pedal, or an audience to appease, but he merely sang just because he had a song in his heart. His song was purer because it refused to stay inside. After a long while, that little black-and-white butcher bird nodded, bobbed a bow in his coat tails and vest, hopped around, stretched his wings and left.

All those times, when people told Ellie she would be famous, or that she had a responsibility to represent their community in song, or insisted it was not just God's gift to her, but also for others... it was too much. All those expectations placed on her in the name of 'encouragement', had also laid the heavy weight of failure on her shoulder because she wasn't famous or exceptional or remarkable. She was just Ellie. Why would God gift her this responsibility? Was it like the gift of little Myrtle, whose death became a curse that changed her mum so completely? Outside one little community choir, every opportunity to pursue music had been taken away because her Mum needed help. That didn't seem like much of a gift. It seemed like God had given it to the wrong person.

Ellie wanted to be more like that little butcher bird, who was faithful in singing his beautiful song regardless of where he was, or what others might think. He would sing magnificently, whether he was sitting on the dirty gutter of their very poor suburban tenement, or whether he was standing in the spotlight on some grand music hall stage. Ellie was certain he would sing just as gloriously, regardless of the setting. As Ellie sat on the rooftop, she found a resolve swelling in her heart to find her song again; to sing like that little bird. She needed to find her own lyrics to sing regardless of what other people thought it should look like, or sound like. The urge to be part of this spontaneous concert with the sparrows bubbled up into her throat and she began to sing. Quietly to start with, but soon one of the grand hymns Marlie had taught her over stringing beans, swelled up into a glorious burst of music from her heart. And she sang it... not because Marlie wanted it, or Miss Lambert at the community hall insisted, or someone else requested it, but she lifted her song to the morning clouds and she allowed it to drift away on the breeze unheard by anyone, except the sparrows and perhaps a little butcher bird. Indeed... how Great Thou art.

* * *

Ellie came in and sat at the table. She placed a watery cup of tea in front of her Mum as she sat with the baby on her knee. "How are you doing Mum?" Ellie asked generically.

"Heard you singing this morning. Haven't heard that in a long time."

"Hmm... I saw a little Butcher bird up there. The way he sang inspired me. I need to do what is good for us Mum and not worry about anybody else."

"Easier said than done, when the whole world is worried. War does that."

"I know. And I have decided that I want to train as a nurse. The war is my chance to do this Mum. It might sound a little opportunistic, but they need people. I was talking to Marlie, and she reckons I will be good at this. She thinks I can get in."

Her mother sat still and said nothing.

"Mum? Please say something. I want you to let me do this."

Eventually her Mum nodded and took another sip of tea. "I knew I could not hold you forever. If it wasn't music, then something else, or someone else, would take you away. I'm just grateful that the boys are too young to enlist. If they were taking on eleven-year-olds, both of them would have signed up already."

"Yeah, I think you are right." Ellie smiled as she looked around their very cramped living room. "Us Pollards are bold and tough and loyal. What we need to do better, is to look out for each other. These are the people who are important to us. I am doing this for us Mum. I am."

"I know." Her Mum blinked into her tea. And she sighed as she recognised she had abdicated her role, and Ellie had stepped into the gap. She always looked out for them. Her mother's heart constricted in fear that she was losing another one of her children, and yet, if Ellie could do this, she could too. She reached out and silently squeezed her daughter's hand in apology and resolve.

* * *

Ellie smoothed her nurses cap and stood by the bed as Sister Perry gave instructions on that fundamental nursing skill: how to make a hospital bed. Ellie stood in the group beside Anna Whitaker. She remembered Anna as the petulant spoilt daughter of Grandfield Park, who quit their afternoon choir practices because she couldn't stand the idea of being one of them. In all the years that Ellie worked with Marlie in the kitchen at Grandfield Park, Anna had never acknowledged her. Not that their paths crossed very often, but when they did, a simple hello would be polite. But then, her silence was telling too.

"What is your name?" Anna whispered to her.

As if she didn't know. Ellie turned away and focused intently on Sister Perry as she spread the sheet over the mattress and folded very tidy hospital corners.

"What's your name?" Anna repeated.

Perhaps she seriously didn't remember. They did look different in their uniforms. Choir practice was a long time ago. And kitchen staff were invisible. "Ellie."

"Ellie. Is that short for something?"

"Just Ellie. Shh. You'll get us in trouble." There goes Annabelle Whitaker with that snobby habit of refusing to shorten names like normal people. No way she was letting anyone know her full name was Elspeth! Eventually she told her just to keep her quiet.

Sister Perry led them into a long ward, and one by one, the beds were emptied of their patients. Anna attached herself to Ellie as her partner as they made their way to their allocated beds. "Don't worry, I used to work for the Auxiliary," said Anna confidently. "I've seen this done a thousand times. What do you think about our first day?" Anna whispered.

"I feel like we are straight into doing real nursing," Ellie whispered back. "I thought it would take longer to get into it."

They began to make the beds. Ellie took great care as she tried to emulate the efficient system imparted to them by Sister Perry. Anna was quizzing Ellie as she practiced her corners. "Have you always wanted to be a nurse? You seem so natural at it all."

Ellie looked up and softened just a little. Perhaps Annabelle Whitaker was more than pouty looks and pretty dresses. A uniform was a great leveller. "I've always looked after my brothers and sisters, so I've had my share of scraped knees and fevers. Helping is something I've always done. Besides... my boyfriend enlisted; I want to help."

"You have boyfriend? Is it serious?"

"I think that..."

Sister Perry appeared out of nowhere and stood over them like a hawk eyeing its prey. "Nurse! No time to chat. You are not here to have tea and scones. Get to work! Both of you show me you can make a bed like a nurse."

Ellie blushed bright red, ducked her head and quickly returned to her starched sheets, precisely folding the corners over the mattress in the prescribed manner. Sister Perry marched back along the end of the beds barking out instructions to her probationary students. Anna shrugged and kept turning down sheets. She could not see that they had done anything that warranted embarrassment. When Sister Perry came back, she stared at their bed. Anna looked up at her buoyantly. "How are we doing Sister?"

Ellie cringed. It sounded impertinent. Being precocious might be cute when you are eleven and wearing muslin tea-dresses. But as a student-nurse on a ward during a global war... everything operated to a different standard.

Sister Perry shook her head and pursed her lips in disgust. She said nothing but reached down and stripped the bed of its linen in a single sweep of her hand. "Do it again. And do it properly!"

Every bed they made that morning was given the same treatment. Just as they were adding a blanket, Sister Perry swooped in and stripped back the bed to the mattress, and they had to start again.

* * *

After that Ellie tried to avoid Anna, but she kept popping up like a creepy Jack-in-the-box toy. Ellie did not need Anna hanging onto her like a limpet. When they had practice exercises, Ellie quickly partnered with any one of the other nursing students to sidestep the awkwardness of being Anna's partner. The other girls objected when they were partnered with Anna as well.

One day, while Ellie was in the dining room with her cup of tea, Anna sat down beside her. Ellie watched Anna screw up her face at her teacup and gag over the thin saltless gravy in the shepherds' pie. Ellie noted that things had not changed that much – nothing was good enough for Annabelle Whitaker. She was still the child who stood aloof in the corner and didn't join in. Ellie continued to eat her meal in silence. Anna put down her cup. "Why don't you want to work with me?" Anna asked her directly.

"I don't know what you mean," said Ellie evasively.

"Yes, you do. You are avoiding me."

Ellie put down her fork. "Well, it just so happens that I remember you, Annabelle Whitaker. And you have always been the

45

one who was avoiding me. But it seems that you have no recollection of that at all."

"We've met? But that's good, isn't it, if we know each other?"

"See... I don't think you understand. You didn't want to notice who I was back then, because I didn't fit your snobby social circle. You don't even seem to realise that I have worked at Grandfield Park for the last six years helping Marlie in the kitchen. But of course, you wouldn't know because you are too high and mighty for us ordinary folk."

Anna stared at her in shock. "You are *that* Ellie, the one Marlie talks about?"

"Apparently, but fortunately for me, snobby doesn't get any points here... only very well-made beds, and accurate observations. Which Sister Perry doesn't seem to think you are able to manage. You are like a cursed penny Annabelle Whitaker. Sister Perry always makes you redo everything. But I need this. I have no back-up plan. My mother cannot subsidise a life of leisure if I fail. Nursing is important to me. Passing my exams, so I can progress to the next level, is important to me. So, I need to protect my progress. And I will. Nothing personal. There is a world out there that is at war, and I will do what I need to do, so that I am able to do my part." Ellie picked up her plate, cup, and cutlery, and moved to another table.

Ellie worked hard, studied diligently and progressed through her levels quickly. She was never required to repeat any lessons.

Perhaps Anna was right: she was a natural. She just kept her head down, studied hard and worked hard. At some point Ellie noticed that she rarely saw Anna anymore, but it was an observation of no import. Ellie was consumed in being the best nurse she could be... and it came easily to her.

* * *

"Sister Pollard?"

Ellie stood up as Matron paused by the desk where she was organising some charts. Matron's face was tired, drawn by the pressure of working and working and working. "Yes Matron?"

"Come to my office at two o'clock." Before she could respond, Matron had already left, walking down the corridor with an efficient tread, belying the fatigue that wracked her body.

Ellie did a quick audit. Had she done everything that needed to be done? Had she missed something? She knew Matron would never leave an urgent matter to address later on, so this had to be something different. At two o'clock, Ellie smoothed her apron, adjusted her glasses and her veil, and then knocked on the door.

Matron barely looked up. "Sister. Take a seat."

"You want me to sit?" Sitting in Matron's office was a deviation from her pattern.

"Yes, just there."

Ellie sat, but on the edge of the chair, so she could bounce to attention on a moment's notice.

Matron finished signing what was in front of her; she set that paper aside and docked her pen. She picked up another form. "I have here your request to be deployed to active service on the war front."

"Yes Ma'am." Ellie's eyes lit up. Finally, she had approval!

"How committed are you to this course?"

"Very Ma'am. The need for medical support is just getting greater. I know I can be of service. I was waiting on my medical clearance. They said my sight might be an issue, but I can assure you Matron, that I can manage the duties."

"Hmm. Sister Pollard, it seems the army disagrees. Given the state of your vision, if something happened to your spectacles, you will be a hindrance, rather than some help. They have declined your application."

"Oh."

"However, I want to propose something. Do you know of the military rehabilitation facility at Grandfield House? I understand that was your old stomping ground."

"Grandfield Park? Yes, I know it well."

"Well, the military is transferring that facility to us. It is now going to be an extension of this hospital, and I am responsible for the staffing. I have reviewed the situation, and it seems that as the military are withdrawing their staff for overseas deployment, we are primarily left with novice nurses, or volunteers who hardly know what they are doing. I need a competent senior nurse who can implement nursing processes efficiently. I know you haven't long graduated, but I want you to take this placement. I can't clear out my already understaffed hospital to man this additional facility. So, because it is rehabilitation rather than acute care, you have what is needed, even though you'll be working with a skeleton staff on a shoe-string budget. It also means you will stay hands-on. Much like what our nurses are doing on the warfront."

Ellie raised her brow. "That is some offer…"

"I consider that this is an exceptional opportunity for someone so young. You will be reporting directly to me, and the facility will have its own doctor to work with the repatriation cases, to rehabilitate them. Although the plan is that patients will return to active duty, the more realistic picture is that those injured seriously enough to be brought back here, will unlikely return to overseas service. Most will stay and serve in the home guard when they are discharged. Your application tells me that you want to serve your country and support those men who have volunteered their lives," stated Matron officially.

Ellie nodded resolutely.

"… then Sister, this posting is a direct line to that cause… just as much as if we were able to give you a place on the next boat deployed overseas."

* * *

Ellie moved into Grandfield and quickly found her feet. She was determined to show the staff that this new arrangement for

50

Grandfield Hospital would enhance the nursing care of the patients. True to Ellie's commitment to Matron's request she was very hands-on. Anything that needed doing, she was in there helping. If that meant rearranging furniture to squeeze another bunk into a room, then Ellie moved the furniture. If it was handing out meals to the patients, she was there – bowls in hand. She already knew the gardener from her kitchen days, a lovely man with a limp, called Mr Hillman... and she often found herself taking her break walking around his herbs and vegetables plots with him as he limped in about his garden beds. "Mr Tiberius Barnes gave me a chance when everyone else thought a man with a limp was useless. That's all these boys need. Someone to believe in them and give them a chance." At other times, she took her breaks with Marlie, standing again at a sink full of dishes, just to talk out some of the challenges she was facing. Marlie's quiet wisdom was something she was pleased to be able to take advantage of once more.

* * *

Ellie lifted the lantern high to distinguish the shadow of a patient stumbling through the corridor, muttering agitatedly. "I have to go! The message! I have to get the signals through!" He had taken off his shirt and was waving it erratically in his delirium.

This was the latest admission. Possible shellshock. 'Standard rehabilitation' they had told her at handover. Ellie watched him duck and weave down the dark corridor. Crouching every so often as he went back and forth across the hallway. This didn't look standard.

"Sir, come back to bed. It is night-time. You don't have to send the message now."

"Oh, but I do... I do!" He pushed her away in his urgency.

"In the morning... when the sun is rising, they will be able to see your signal. Let's try that. It is dark now. You need to rest."

"But it cannot be put off! It is most urgent!"

"I know... I know. Come with me, I can help with that... this way..." She whispered urgently and grabbed his hand. "This way. Shhh. Be quiet. We don't want them seeing us."

The man stared at her through the dim shadows and then tilted his sculptured jawline and nodded efficiently; he had an ally in this terrible situation where he found himself. "Quietly now. This is the tricky part..." said Ellie looking at him curiously. There was something familiar about him. But in the shadows, she couldn't place where or when, so she directed him back to his stretcher and slipped a powder into is tumbler before she offered it to him. "I know the water tastes funny, but it is clean. Try and drink it all..."

He drained the cup as he sat restlessly on the bunk. She sat quietly with him until she felt him relax. The scars down the side of his thin torso were red and raised but healing well enough. She felt his forehead; he was burning up, so she didn't put his shirt back on and had him lie down on top of the covers. Ellie went into the other room and brought back the fan that was shared between the wards. She sat it on the chair beside the patient, but the buzzing and clinking of the fan caused him to restlessly start to twitch and duck again. She turned it off and grabbed a magazine and gently blew a breeze across his sweaty torso.

She retrieved the chart for Bed 4B from the nurses' station. She stared at the name as she sat by his bed. Philip Sinclair? She shook her head, raised her lamp, and looked at the patient in the shadows. Flip Sinclair? She couldn't help noticing that he looked so different from the kid racked with asthma, beaten up by the neighbourhood bullies. This was a long way from being dunked in the horse trough. The man in the corridor was determined to fulfill his duty in face of all the danger he had faced, real or imagined, yet he still pushed through. She adjusted her glasses and read through his chart by the light of the lantern, going over his notes, entry by entry.

He had enlisted in the signaller's corps; saw active duty; was wounded and shipped out. His hospital ship had survived a surface attack and limped into a nearby allied port. His original injuries were healing, but his mental state deteriorated and continued to be variable and unstable. Shellshock was the official diagnosis. Ellie pursed her lips. She knew the stigma that surrounded patients with shellshock: they were either putting it on, or crazy, but mostly the tone around the condition was that these soldiers were weak, not taking their duty seriously, or using this as a way to escape their responsibilities.

None of that sounded like Flip. He was the most loyal of people. Tough in his own quiet, unassuming way. Every choir practice he would turn up and hand out their books. Shyness aside. He was always there. That was something she was confident would not change. Shellshock did not give patients fevers, but his fever could be compounding his delirium. She checked the scars on his side again and was confident they were healing well. She went through the chart again in case there was something she had missed and could highlight to the doctor. Doctor Redmond was a very reasonable man.

She monitored Flip's temperature all night. Running from his bed to other patients as other calls demanded her attention. On dawn his fever broke, and he lay in his sheets, restless and sweaty, still murmuring about messages that needed to be sent. Light leaked through the window. It had been a long time since Ellie had a frantic shift like that. She was finishing changing the sweat drenched sheets on Flip's bed when Rex in the next bed quietly lifted his hand. She looked over at him as he quietly murmured, "I hear singing..." She frowned and stood still for a moment as they listened to the sparrows outside, chirping and whistling their greeting for the day. She tilted her head as she remembered how she used to join their chorus every morning; it had been her rule: greet the day with a morning song. She took a deep breath, cleared her throat and did a few warmups. "Hmm–Hmm–Ahhh!" She took another breath. "Hmm–Hmm–Ahhh!" She followed up by humming a scale or two. Miss Lambert said her voice was an instrument that needed tuning before playing, every time, without exception. "Hmm–Hmm–Ahhh!"

She looked across at Flip and he lay there on his fresh sheets with a tense frown on his face, tired and drawn from the battles he had fought all night. He tilted his head and nodded faintly. "Hmm – Hmm – Ahhh..." and he sat up. She went to settle him again but instead he squared his shoulders. "Hmm – Hmm – Ahhh..." Ellie repeated it and curiously watched him hum and sigh in time with her. Again, he followed her cue. "Hmm–Hmm–Ahhh!" She kept the rhythm going for some time, then she ran a couple of scales... "Doh, Re, Mi, Fa, Sol, La, Ti, Doh." His face relaxed, as his rich baritone ran the scales with her. Ellie quietly sang the verse of a familiar ballad and watched as his breathing settled into a quiet pattern, and after the chorus, he relaxed back on his pillow and was soon sleeping.

She continued to gently hum as she went over to the next bed. "Rex, I am so sorry that your night was so disturbed," she whispered.

"He's had a hard time of it. Seen what you did there though. First time I've seen him relax since he came in. You've got magic in that voice of yours. Haven't heard anything like that for quite a while..."

"Well, I'm not a proponent of magic... but faith and hope... these are things that have power to heal."

Rex nodded. "We can all do with a bit of hope..."

She smiled as she put away her thermometer and straightened his bed before she moved on to the next patient. "I believe that too."

* * *

When Ellie came into the kitchen, she found Miss Lambert and Marlie sitting at the bench sipping lemongrass tea. The war rations made straight traditional British tea a luxury, but rather than miss their daily cuppas altogether, Marlie improvised with her own versions of tea. They used to have a Chinese gardener at Grandfield who loved his herbal teas. So, while the rest of the nation jealously guarded tea-coupons, Marlie bulked out her rations of tea leaves with blends of basil or lemongrass or mint from Mr Hillman's amazing herb garden by drying leaves from his herb plants in the sun, or in the warming oven.

Marlie looked up with a glorious smile. "Will you join us Sister Pollard for a cup of tea. Today's blend is lemongrass refreshing and sharp."

Ellie offered a tired smile. "Refreshing sounds good.. especially with two of my favourite people. How could I say no?" Suddenly Ellie gripped the side of the table, her head spinning, an exhausted sigh escaped her lips.

Marlie quickly guided her to a chair and sat her down. She filled up her cup from the teapot sitting on the trivet, dressed in its tea-cosy. "You look quite beat, my Dear," she said quietly.

"Hmm. I am. But I also know it comes with the territory. I have to endure no more than any solider fighting for our liberty. And I have the comfort of a bed, excellent food and good friends around me."

"My Dear, have you considered that if you run yourself ragged, to the point of falling over, then you jeopardise the hospital. We need you to be healthy, not worn so thin that you can hardly move. These patients rely on you."

Ellie shook her head. "Caring is not hard work. Not really. These people have been through hell. They need me to be available for them."

Ellie was soon draining her teacup and stood up.

Miss Lambert nodded. "Would you mind singing a song with me Ellie before you go? One of our favourites. Just for old times sake..."

"Oh Miss Lambert, I really don't..." She looked at her familiar kind eyes and relented. "Well okay... perhaps a chorus..."

Miss Lambert smiled delightedly and named her piece as she stood up. Without waiting for warm-ups, she launched into the song. Ellie blinked. When did Miss Lambert ever break her own rules? She went to join her, but instead stood there with her mouth open, her eyes wide. Eventually she sat while Miss Lambert kept singing another verse and another chorus... the notes blurred, the rhythm was off, the tempo was fast, the melody was lost. And when she finished, she sat down and took up her cup of tea. "I remember that was one of your favourite songs. Did you enjoy it Dear?"

"It was... interesting..." Barely recognisable.

"Oh? Interesting? You didn't enjoy it? But why? I sang every lyric and note with gusto."

Ellie went to say something and then sadly smiled and slumped her shoulders just a little. "Clever Miss Lambert. Very clever."

She raised her eyebrows innocently. "I am merely a singer. Please, tell me... what did you notice? Why didn't it sound right?"

Ellie nodded and slowly acknowledged the parable. "You are correct... the notes and lyrics were accurate individually, but you didn't hold them as they were written. The tempo was higher, and you ignored the rests. It sounded terrible."

Miss Lambert reached out and held her hand. "My Dear, you have the capacity to make your work here, a musical masterpiece. But if you override the basic principles of tempo and rest, it will not be remembered for anything other than a cacophony of noise. Instead, make this something that people want to carry with them. Bring your theory of music into everything that you do. That must always mean tempo and rest."

"Tempo and rest," Ellie echoed. Marlie wordlessly poured Ellie another cup of tea, as she picked up her cup quietly with tears in her eyes. "Tempo and rest." Then she chuckled and took off her glasses and swiped her lids. "You're a genius really... singing like that! I would find it quite impossible."

"Committed might be more accurate. You are committed too, but it is stealing your melody. You can do it either way... it is your decision. Ellie, which sort of song do you want to be known for?"

She blinked as she stood up. That question. It echoed of another question, from another time, but she couldn't remember exactly what it was. "You have given me a lot to think about Ladies. Duties calls." And walked briskly to her office, with the official air of a ward sister and then closed the door. She bent over her desk, her breathing coming fast and raspy. Eventually she stood up and squared her shoulders. "Hmm–Hmm–Ahhh! Hmm–Hmm–Ahhh!" Which sort of song *did* she want to be known for? Tempo and Rest. Tempo and Rest. The melody of the butcherbird was the purer sound.

She was still Miss Lambert's lamb, who had again been shepherding her choir, using her baton to correct her breathing, and her tempo, without neglecting the pauses and rests. Ellie needed to be mindful on how to metre her tempo and rest, not just for herself and her staff, but also her patients. Miss Lambert was right... this driven pace was not helping her patients find the melody of what life could be again. For most of these men, the war was over. They were not going back.

Ellie was reminded of Rex's husky, tired morning voice patiently acknowledging the war still raged for most of them. "He's had a hard time of it. Seen what you did there though. First time I've seen him relax since he came in. We can all do with a bit of hope."

She found herself going back to the quiet wisdom of Mr Hillman as he limped around his garden. The military-driven targets demanding soldiers rehabilitate and achieve the same level of capacity as they had with whole limbs and full eyesight, would just impose judgements of acquired incompetency and failure. Being here was no fault of theirs. What Ellie wanted was to give them that second chance... to have programs that would introduce them to the practices of tempo and rest. That balance between going fast and pausing in stillness. That might include gardening, tennis, music and art lessons or even a men's choir. And she would invite the army chaplain to offer, not just the usual visitation, but sessions on prayer and meditation. She would heed the requests for a song to start the day and close the day with a ballad before dinner. Yes, she was going to bring tempo and rest into this sombre, clinical, painful place that once was someone's home. She might not be able to do all this herself, but she would fight to bring back the music.

* * *

8

Ellie picked up a pile of charts and stood to attention as the doctor came to her side. "Sister, are you ready for our rounds."

"Yes Doctor."

But he didn't rush. "How are your patients? Any concerns that I need the heads-up about?"

"Oh. Yes actually. We have had a few new admissions. There is one soldier, who worked as a signalman. Has come in with shellshock. There are some wounds across his chest and side, but they all seem to be healing well. However, he does have a history of asthma."

Dr Redmond adjusted his spectacles and looked over the notes. "I see that you have noted his asthma, but I can't find this in his notes prior to your entries. It doesn't seem he was in any coherent state to gather a verbal history. Have you just made a reasonable guess about this?"

"No, actually there was no need to guess Doctor. But you are right: it wasn't in his notes. I recognised Mr Sinclair as a childhood friend. We used to sing in a community choir together."

"Choir? You sing?"

"I do... and it is something I need to do more often. A place like this needs music."

"That is something I agree with..."

Ellie noted his support of something outside the sombre tradition of medical facilities and quickly directed the doctor's attention back to the patient. "He was given strict singing exercises that were intended to strengthen his breathing. And they did. But given the history of weakness in his lungs, do you think it is possible he has pneumonia? That could account for his fever. He is not coughing much... but he has been too agitated or me to listen to his chest."

"Well Sister, if he is your childhood friend, let's give him a thorough check."

Ellie shook her head. "I would like to think we give every patient thorough care... childhood companions or not."

"Ahh. So, this Mr Sinclair was your childhood sweetheart?"

"Flip? Oh no. My other boyfriend would never allow it!" she said with a laugh, to cover the blush on her cheeks. "His name was Billy."

"Oh my. The companionship of Sister Pollard, was very much sought after."

"Not as much as you make it sound."

"So, is this Billy still in the picture?" Doctor Redmond continued, flipping through another chart, eyeing her curiously from over the rim of his eyeglasses.

"He enlisted, and I became a nurse. Doctor, you do know that nurses are not allowed to date. I have not heard from either of them since they left the neighbourhood to enlist, until now." This ignorance was not a burden, but a relief... especially when it came to Billy.

"I understood that nurses could date, but when they marry, they leave their profession. If they want to stay connected to their work that is the problem."

"Exactly. There is a war on. Our work is the priority." Ellie picked up the pile of charts and pointed down the hallway as she led the way to Flip's room. "There is absolutely no value in starting something that could never be finished."

"I am pretty sure I could think of a few valuable reasons," he said with a charming smile. Then he pointed to the chart in his hand. "Sister, do you know how Mr Sinclair managed his asthma sufficiently to pass a military medical assessment?"

"Just what I mentioned about the community choir. The local doctor prescribed singing lessons, and our music teacher had a very vigorous routine of vocal and breathing exercises. I understand that is how he got through the medical."

Dr Redmond looked thoughtful. "I hope you are wrong about the pneumonia. If that is the case, there is not a lot we can do, except pray. But if he is already familiar with the breathing exercises, then I will prescribe them as well. Do those routines with him twice a day, three times if you can fit it in. And if you can add in a song, I'm sure the patients will not be too distressed to hear you sing more often. I know I won't."

"You flatter me Dr Redmond."

"It is not flattery, if it is honest." Ellie handed him a chart as they continued their rounds.

A slamming door would send Flip scurrying for cover; the clanging of a dropped metal bowl would cause him to lose any sense of the present; the echoes of trolly wheels on the hard timber floors would send him straight back to the battlefield. With the daily prescription of exercises Flip steadily improved. Ellie included her warm-ups while attending to Flip's morning observations and making his bed, so that they would go through the prescribed exercises together. Flip would sit by the bed and run the vocal exercises with her as she worked, and then they would finish with a duet together. Flip would naturally step into harmonising with her. Afterward, he would lie back down with a smile on his face and a sigh in his heart. Rex heard him say many times, "I can't believe I get to sing with Ellie Pollard again."

The patients would gather as they did this morning routine and it was so popular that Ellie included a routine at dinnertime where she would start with a song before they said Grace, blessing their meal in prayer. Each time the soldiers would clang their cutlery and cry for an encore. And each time she would smile and nod and decline. She was choosing which song she would be known for.

* * *

"Sister, the new admissions have arrived." Ellie was handed a clipboard and a pile of charts and paperwork.

Ellie scanned the list of diagnoses and then ran her finger over their names. Her finger stopped suddenly over one name. William Stamford. "Billy? Here?" she murmured quietly. "Surely not." It was not that long ago she had spoken his name, and now he was here. Her chest constricted, and her heart started to beat faster. A feeling of dread spread from her chest leaching into the pit of her stomach, sinking there like a dark toxic sludge. She had dreamed of being with someone whom she longed to see, praying they would return home, safe and unharmed. The newspaper often ran stories of reunited sweethearts. Not this. She hadn't realised until now that this war had been her freedom, and suddenly she was under fire again. She took a deep breath. "Hmm–Hmm–Ahhh!" Flip had helped to remember how effective these exercises were, and not just for singing. She repeated it a few times until she noticed the tightness in her throat relax.

Ellie did her rounds, checked on all the new admissions, and approved their rehabilitation plans. She paused at the door, and watched Billy lying on his bunk, bandages over the side of his face, that only partly covered abrasions across his nose and cheeks. Notes

65

on his chart stated that his left ear had been blown off. Part of one arm and one leg were also missing. Ellie went around to the other side of the bed and stood there for a moment. "Billy...? It's Ellie. Do you know where you are?"

His eyes opened and Ellie shuffled back. Recognition was quickly replaced by the rage that filled his face. "I'm in hell. That's where!"

Ellie took a breath and spoke evenly. "You are in Grandfield Hospital. We have a good rehabilitation program here. I am the Sister-in-Charge. The nurses will make sure you are well looked after."

Billy swore at her. "I'm not having just anyone look after me! You are my girl. You're doing it! No one else." Another volley of obscenities spewed from his mouth.

Ellie took a breath. She needed to prune back that particular thought straight away, right from the get-go. She stood firm. "Billy, I cannot be 'your girl' here. Not anymore. I am the Sister-in-charge, so I cannot be anyone's girlfriend, much less a patient's. There are rules about these things. But this doesn't mean we won't look after you well. All our patients get the best care."

He swore again, yelling out his assertion. "Just because you got a job don't change the fact you are my girl, Ellie Pollard! Can't change what is. And believe me when I say it – that won't ever change. It especially won't change even when I heard 'em say I'm only half a man now! But I reckon even my half is better than any other bloke who survived this war. So, you'd better not be seeing anyone else. You know I mean it! I've said it before... I can do it again."

Ellie shook her head. "Billy, we are not kids anymore roaming the streets, where you can strong arm your way around. We have to be clear about the line between our designations. You are to call me Sister Pollard, and I will call you Mr Stamford while you are a patient."

"Like hell I will... *Ellie.*" He stared at her with a wild dare in his eye poking out from the bandages.

"The nurses will look after your needs Mr Stamford. Good day." Ellie walked out of the room and leant up against the wall in the corridor for a moment. She took a shaky breath. It felt spineless to hide behind her nurses' uniform. Whether it was a cowardly thing to do or not, she would use that for as long as she needed to. This was the most accessible shield available to her.

"Sister Pollard?"

She looked up quickly. "Oh... Flip. Are you okay?"

Concern creased his brow. "I... umm... I heard... umm... I heard what Billy was saying to you. Well, we all did... he was very... loud. And I think you are right. I think it is best to keep everything separate... to avoid confusion. So, I will be doing that as well, so he doesn't think our arrangement is different."

"Oh. I see."

"Yes Ma'am... Sister. I would like you to call me Philip if you would... or Mr Sinclair. I am probably too old for Flip now anyways.'

"Sure Flip...Philip... Mr Sinclair... yes, thank you." She thrust out her hand to shake on it. He grabbed it eagerly, twisting his grip into that very awkward hold that sealed their private pact of friendship so long ago.

"Thank you, Sister Pollard. Don't forget... some things won't ever change."

Ellie smiled and squeezed his hand gratefully. "I agree with you on that, Mr Sinclair," she said warmly.

Ellie was certain that Billy Stamford was not bluffing. Billy was writhing in a swamp of burbling rage over his pain and disability. She had supported grief and loss in this place every day, and experience told her that was an unstable and difficult place for any man, but for those with Billy's temperament, it was a perilous and unpredictable volatile combination. She reported her cautionary concerns to her nursing staff; authorised the use of restraints if he was aggressive and made a note to check-in with Dr Redmond to have additional sedation prescribed *Pro re Nata... P.R.N.*, to be used if circumstances require it.

* * *

9

Doctor Redmond wrote out the prescription, and as he was leaving the nurses station, he paused and pulled Ellie aside. "Sister Pollard," he said gravely, "may I have a word?"

She looked at him quickly. "Yes Doctor?"

"I need to ask your opinion on quite a serious matter," he said grimly.

"Sure," she said, scanning her patients in her mind, like thumbing through a well-referenced notepad. Had Billy consumed so much of her thinking, that she had missed something significant for other patients? Perhaps the Doctor needed further clarification regarding Billy's threats, or more detail on Billy's history. "Ask away."

"Will you come out with me... for a coffee or a meal sometime?"

"Oh? This is not a clinical question... not a reprimand?"

His eyes smiled, amplified through his lenses. "Not unless you say 'No'. Then it would require a reprimand. I did say this was a serious matter."

"Oh." She smiled noncommittally.

"Oh? I think I am a little offended that you don't have a more enthusiastic response than that for me."

"But in this situation, there is a more serious consideration. Just now you were writing that prescription for Billy Stamford for those very sober reasons. I am certain this is not a good idea. Billy can be quite vindictive if he sets his mind to it. I do not want to put you in the firing line. You've already done your stint of fighting on the war front. This placement should not put you in any further danger."

"Sister, I think you underestimate the effective combination of sedation and restraints. Both of which will provide adequate protection and security to enhance the patient's recovery."

"I know you want to rationalise this... but Billy can be pretty riled up. Just now he is in a constant state of agitation. I don't trust him not to make the situation much bigger than it really is."

"Well, my professional assessment is that I think we have *that* small situation sorted. Yet still, you still hesitate?"

"You wanted my opinion, and it is that I am not convinced it is only a 'small' situation. And on top of that I am getting used to the idea..."

"What idea?

"The idea that you would want to... you know... keep company with me."

"What is there not to want? Sister Pollard... Ellie... you meet every quality I have dreamed of in a girl. You are kind, and intelligent, and your pretty smile is probably only outshone by your stunning voice. Your diligence in that particular prescription has done this place a world of good."

"Ahh. My voice." It was always about her voice.

"It is not surprising that your beautiful voice would be famous... not only with the patients, but it is building a reputation outside the hospital as well. Did you know they've dubbed this place 'The Singing Hospital'?"

Ellie nodded; she had heard that too. But she didn't consider it an insult. This was exactly what she had been working towards.

Doctor Redmond raised his brow and waited for her to respond to his invitation. Still, she hesitated. "I find it curious that you only heard me say I admire your voice. Did you not notice that I started with kind and intelligent?" he said gently. "And don't forget pretty."

Ellie took a deep breath. "You are right. You did say that. I'm sorry. I have spent my entire life, being fought over because I can sing. I have often wondered if that is the only thing of value that people think I have to offer."

"Well, I appreciate identify with the idea of constantly being fought over... much more than you probably realise. I can't deny I enjoy listening to you sing, but it is definitely not the only thing I admire."

"Well Doctor Redmond, your confidence is encouraging. I get off at eleven-thirty tonight... so if you are not too tired, and still inclined to go for a walk, then meet me in front of the Glasshouse. Walking around the garden is a way for me to wind-down after my shift."

"I will be there." He paused and turned back to her with a gentle nod. "See you at eleven-thirty Ellie."

Ellie escaped down the stairs. She had been held up by several matters, but finally, her shift was over. She jolted as she saw Doctor Redmond standing by the Glasshouse. She hadn't really believed he would wait for her. He was in smart civilian clothes and looked very relaxed, even while he was waiting. How remarkable that this likeable doctor was interested in her. Just the girl next door, who had been labelled as a local celebrity, but who always felt like a fraud because she didn't deserve the accolades that were piled on her by local loyalists.

Ellie took a deep breath of the outside garden air. She could smell the jasmine and hear the night crickets and an occasional bird calling through the dark. To be outside was the most effective way she had found to wind-down after a busy shift. Doctor Redmond gallantly bowed and swept his arm forward as they fell in step along the compacted gravel path. Ellie's pace was strong as she walked out the residual tension from her day. "You seem wired. Are you okay?" he asked softly.

"I will be. If I don't walk, I don't sleep, and then tomorrow is harder than it needs to be. I find that I walk faster to start with, then

I can ease back until I feel relaxed and calm. It may seem like a strange prescription to a medical doctor, but this is a routine that suits me."

"Not strange. It bears the marks of remarkable self-awareness. It is good you take the liberty do the things that suit you."

"I appreciate you saying that, Doctor Redmond."

"Alfred... please. It is appropriate that you call me that while off duty. I have taken off my doctors' coat... intentionally I might add. We are not at work now."

They walked for a long time, talking about the things that brought them together. So many things had converged to create this moment in the Grandfield night garden. It seemed strange to think of their walk in those terms. Destiny assigning this moment of togetherness. Gradually, Ellie's pace eased, and they now sauntered with quiet laughter and relaxed jokes.

Alfred looked into her eyes sparkling in the night shadows. They seemed to have a light of their own. He gently leant into kiss her lips, when there was a loud skuttle close by that made them both jump. Alfred stopped and pulled Ellie off the path. "Shh. Someone is here."

Ellie giggled. "You do know that staff are still settling after their shifts. We are not the only ones who do this."

"No, I could swear it was a patient."

"A patient? Who? You don't think it is Billy, do you?" A lump that refused to be swallowed constricted her throat. Her chest started to pound, and the hair on her arms prickled.

"Not sure. He went this way..." He grabbed Ellie's hand, and they crouched behind the bushes as they spotted the white nightgown of the man ducking through the trees. Definitely a patient. "Any ideas who that is?" he asked in a whisper.

She let out a sigh and relaxed. "Not Billy. He is moving too freely. Actually... I could guarantee that is Flip Sinclair. Flip is the signalman who is still fighting battles loyally in name of King and Country. I find that remarkable, given that Flip has always been a pacifist by nature. Or perhaps that is why the fighting still haunts him."

"I think our battles still haunt all of us, Ellie," said Alfred soberly. They kept to the shadows and followed Flip as he ducked in and out between the trees.

"Well, I appreciate your understanding. Not all staff are so amendable to the plight of these soldiers. Lose a leg, and you are a hero. Lose your sense of time and place, and you are a coward. It is a harsh judgement that is undeserved."

They moved forward and spotted Flip crouching behind a tree breathless and sweaty.

Ellie moved closer. "Psst! Flip! It's Ellie. Come back! Come over here!" she whispered.

Flip's eyes flickered and blinked. "Ellie? What are you doing out here? Keep down. It is dangerous."

"Just looking out for you. Come over here. I need you."

They were magical words. She needed him. He jumped up and scuttled to her side. Flip stared at the Doctor, who spoke softly, reassuring him. "Hi Soldier. I'm Doctor Redmond. Do you know my friend Ellie?"

Ellie blushed at his acknowledgment of friendship. She felt her chest flutter and was grateful that the night shadows covered the heat rising in her face.

Flip didn't blink. "Everyone knows Ellie. She is the prettiest and kindest girl in all the neighbourhood."

The doctor chuckled. "I'd have to agree with you there."

Ellie shook her head. That was like Flip not to say she had the prettiest voice. She liked that about him. He saw past the performance to who she really was. "What are you doing out here Flip... Philip?"

"I was testing these new eyeglasses that you organised for me...". He chuckled as if he had noticed a huge joke. Flip's glasses were standard army issue with round tortoiseshell rims. "Look at us. All three of us wear spectacles now... "Anyway... I saw him through the window as clear as anything. You have really help me. Now I have to help him."

"Who did you see? Who are you looking for?"

"Captain Whitaker," he said matter-of-factly, looking around the shadows. "I saw him walking through the garden."

"Oh. Captain Whitaker... as in Max Whitaker, who used to live here at Grandfield Park?"

"Yes! He saved my life, and now I have to help him. I must help him! He's wounded."

"Well, that is very honourable of you Flip... I mean Philip. But Captain Whitaker is not a patient here."

"Oh, but I saw him. I did. He was with a nurse. I have to help him!"

Doctor Redmond looked at him curiously and cleared his throat. "Soldier, you do know that Sister Pollard would know all the patients admitted in the hospital. If she says he is not a patient than that is the case. She is the sister-in-charge."

Ellie knew telling Flip otherwise would just aggravate his delusion. "I'll tell you what... tomorrow when I'm on the ward, I will check the records again. Just now, we need to get you back to bed. Come... get some rest and we will look at it tomorrow. I promise. You have my word."

"Oh Ellie, this is very important. Captain Whitaker spent a lot of time looking out for others; he deserves to have someone looking out for him... at a time like this."

"Having someone look out for us is always important Philip. Let's get back..."

Alfred couldn't help feeling a twang of disappointment as Ellie cut short their walk for a patient. Still, loyalty to her job was another quality in her favour. He said his goodnights and quietly retreated as Ellie soothed Flip's anxious distress with the calm of her voice and guided him back to the ward.

* * *

10

It became a routine that Ellie looked forward to. Walking out the stress of the day with the amiable Doctor Redmond, with his kind blue eyes and gentle manner. Sometimes Ellie finished early, and they walked in the evening... just on sunset. At other times it was late in the night, long after the changeover with the nightshift before all her duties were done. Whatever the time, Alfred would be there. Sometimes the anticipation of these nightly garden walks was all the respite she had to look forward to. He would offer a listening ear as they debriefed their day together. Ellie got used to looking for Philip darting through the garden searching for Captain Whitaker. She found it comforting in a way. It felt like he was looking out for her too: a kind figure from a past life who kept popping up to remind her of his friendship. Rarely did she need to escort him back to the ward now, but a quiet word of reassurance and encouragement would send him returning to his bed. She also got used to not worrying about Billy. Alfred created a bubble of safety around her.

Almost without exception they talked about patients, treatments and programs. Alfred avoided any topic to do with his life outside of Grandfield, but as the doctor unapologetically pointed out, this work was their common ground; their shared experience; their mutual passion. Every so often, Alfred would slow the pace of their walking. "You know Ellie Pollard, you are not like any girl I have known. I cannot overstate how much I enjoy our walks and honest talks together. You are a breath of fresh air that is blowing over the stale air of the world out there. Thank you." Ellie and Alfred worked well together and were quickly becoming fast friends, even more than friends, as they walked the paths together.

This evening was not particularly special. Or at least it didn't seem so. They were talking about adjusting their programs to support the 'Limbies' more effectively. They chuckled over the nickname 'Limbies' which the soldiers good-naturedly adopted to those adjusting to life with prosthetics. They had installed an obstacle course beside the tennis court, stepping over logs and on platforms at various heights to help them practise judging distance and placement. More than one solider came a cropper trying to navigate this course using their artificial legs. They encouraged Limbies to play tennis to help practice balance and mobility. Ellie wanted to offer other practical pathways to help soldiers reabsorb back into civilian life as they were discharged from the army on medical grounds. Sometimes trying to make any sort of decision was overwhelming, because, as each man enlisted, so many choices had been stripped away from them. Ellie was explaining some training opportunities she was exploring, about re-skilling into other vocations, like book-keeping, shopkeeping, or some artisan workshops like leatherwork and woodturning. She had found some businesses who would donate typewriters and cash-registers for use in this program, and she had ideas on who she could approach to come in as tutors. She would talk to Tibby about remodelling the stables, knocking out the dividers between stalls, so the separated spaces could be set up for each specific workshop.

Ellie and Alfred were immersed in the pros and cons of expanding the program, hardly pausing to admire the evening light in the garden, when suddenly a figure came barrelling across the path; a prosthetic leg and arm swinging wildly. He tackled Alfred to the ground like a maniac and started beating into him in a menacing frenzy. Ellie shrieked and tried to pull him off, but he swung hard and slogged her with his wooden arm. She fell hard on the gravel path. She raised her eyes, barely able to whisper through the paralysing blur. "Billy... Stop... Billy stop!" She was back on the street watching someone she loved being pummelled by Billy Standford. People swarmed to smother him in a pile of weighted bodies. Someone ran for back-up, as Ellie lay paralysed by the hysteria that overwhelmed her, immobilised by horror and anguish. When the wardsmen finally arrived, the pile of people peeled away so they were able to sedate and subdue Billy and carry him off. Alfred lay limp and unresponsive on the dew drenched grass stained with his blood. Ellie crawled to his side and fell across his body moaning. Gentle hands lifted her back, pressed her glasses into her hand and she fell into those arms sobbing as they loaded Alfred onto a gurney and ferried him away. She didn't even register that it was Philip who held her.

* * *

Everything blurred. Ellie had been trying to find companionship and meaning in an isolating and meaningless war. It seemed that as soon as she was gaining some sort of traction, Billy pushed the bottom out of her life again. No... that sounded too moderate. Billy tore gashes in it until it bled out.

She walked around the garden, numbed by pain. She stopped and swallowed her tears, as she passed by that spot. She hadn't realised. She went to quickly hurry on, when she saw a glint in the grass. She picked up Alfred's bent and shattered spectacle frames. She crumpled in a heap and sobbed and sobbed, holding them to her chest.

Billy was arrested and court martialled. The charges of causing grievous bodily harm were firm and were added to a long rap-sheet of insubordination, theft and assault. Attempted murder was on the table and there was the reality of it being upgraded to some degree of murder if Alfred did not pull through. Alfred was transferred to a larger private hospital, in a coma. Ellie was required to give several statements, including the circumstances of her initial assessment that prompted her to ask Dr Redmond to prescribe Private William Stamford a sedative, and an investigation surrounding the circumstances of his ability to get out of the ward unsupervised was initiated.

Someone sent her flowers. Another bouquet of beauty when life had been snuffed out. No matter who she asked, no one could give any specific hope regarding Alfred's prognosis. All enquiries Ellie made were stonewalled. She begged for time off so that she could go across to the other hospital to visit him. She stood outside the ward watching staff rush to-and-fro. This was no different to the places she had worked, but as she stood there, this moment was suspended in a type of out-of-body experience. Eventually a nurse paused and asked if she needed help. When Ellie said she had come to visit Doctor Alfred Redmond, the nurses' eyes widened a little and referred her immediately to the Ward Sister.

"You have come to visit Doctor Redmond?" the sister asked suspiciously staring at her grazed face and arms, and her very ordinary town-dress.

"Yes. He was... he is my friend."

The Sister looked at her. Patiently. "I think you know that only family gets to visit patients in such a precarious condition."

"I know... but we... well, we were... engaged." Almost. It was definitely headed in that direction. And she knew she had to pull out some sort of legitimate connection if she would be allowed to see him.

"Engaged? You are his fiancé? Why didn't you say so? The family said they were waiting for you to arrive." She nodded and signalled Ellie to follow her. She was ushered into a darkened room. Ellie looked around confused. It was filled with flowers. Soldiers all over the world were struggling to be even allocated a stretcher, and here was one man being given all the care of a celebrity, easily absorbing the resources they would use for ten men at Grandfield.

A lady sat by his bed. Her fashionable clothes screamed wealth and privilege. After years of being immersed in khaki and shades of drab olive green, it was strange to see this woman sitting by Alfred's bed dressed as if she was going to the opera with Miss Lambert. Her eyes narrowed as Ellie tentatively stepped forward.

"Good afternoon. I have come to see how Alfred is... after..." Ellie's voice trailed off as the woman severely stared at her, up and down.

"I am Mrs Redmond. His mother. And you are...?"

"Ellie Pollard, Ma'am. I was... am... a friend of Alfred's."

"We have never seen you before." She frowned as she considered the bruises and grazes on her face and arms.

"No, I understand. However, Alfred and I worked closely together." Their hearts had connected. Every evening. Theirs was a unique and special friendship. They talked about everything.

"Humph. So, you are a nurse. That is not surprising. It is a matter of dressing up common Help to make it look like sort of virtue. Do you know who Alfred is?"

"He was the doctor at Grandfield Hospital. His approach to rehabilitation was very innovative. I was with him when..."

"That barbaric place couldn't keep its inmates in check! I really don't think it is appropriate that you are here. I have specifically asked that only family be allowed to visit."

"I... I wanted to see that he had his spectacles back." Ellie passed over the frames wrapped in a clean simple handkerchief. She knew what it was like to see life as a blur. She didn't know what else to say.

His mother took them. "They are useless anyway," she said dismissively.

As Ellie tried to gather her thoughts, another young lady came through the door. Her clothes were only slightly less pretentious than his mother's.

"Oh, my dear Mrs Redmond," the young woman gushed. "I came as soon as I heard. This is a nightmare."

"Evelyn-Rose! My Dear, I am so grateful you are finally here. You do know Alfred regards you so very fondly even if the war interfered with his plans for a formal proposal. This is exactly the prescription he needs. I feel much more hopeful now that you have arrived.

Mrs Redmond passed her the glasses to Evelyn-Rose and stared at them. "What are they doing here?"

"The nurse brought them."

"They shouldn't be here," she said, and hurriedly put them away as if she was hiding evidence. "I cannot believe what your family went through to keep Alfred off the boats. Failing a medical screen hardly seems worthwhile now. Not if it means he was to be attacked like this right in our own back yard. He might as well have gone to the warfront if that was the outcome. This is unbelievable!"

"I'm sure he will quickly improve now that he has his beloved bethrothed with him."

"Betrothed? You are engaged?" Ellie gasped. Ellie shook her head. There was too much information flying around the room. Had she known Alfred at all?

"Of course. Surely, you didn't have ambitions of joining the Redmond circle? You are just one of many naive hopeful women who had stars in their eyes. Alfred is a gentle soul, so much like his father in that respect, but personally I think it is kinder to just firmly put such aspirations to bed right from the start."

The two women continued to talk and no longer acknowledged that Ellie was in the room. She turned to leave. Tears stung the back of her throat, burning with shame. How could she not have known any of this? Didn't he say that he enjoyed their walks and honest talks? *Honest?* Mrs Redmond was right. There was a lot she didn't know; he hadn't been entirely honest. What is left unspoken can be more telling than what is frankly disclosed. Alfred never corrected any of the assumptions she had made that he had returned from active duty overseas. It was offensive that he never actually left Australian soil when he could have legitimately supported those who needed his skill over there! How many lives would that have saved? The stale air of the world that Alfred had alluded to, was evidently not the horror of war as she thought. It was entirely possible he was referring to the musty air of another version of Grandfield, which had not yet caught up with a world that was irrevocably changing. In that, she believed Alfred had been entirely honest. She was the fresh air blowing over his life that he had been craving. Well, that window just slammed shut.

She might have been a distraction, or a diversion, or even a workplace fling. Perhaps she would never really know exactly what Alfred's intentions were. Not knowing and uncertainty were part of the fall out of war, like those chloride gas clouds blowing over their troops fighting in trenches where their only tenuous protection was wearing those terrifying and vile gas masks. Whoever Ellie thought Alfred was, she finally conceded he had worn his own mask. In the end, placebo eyeglasses were no protection at all. She never saw who he really was... and now he was gone, even if he lay in a hospital bed. She had to let him go. She didn't have the strength to go back to work, fight for his recovery, as well as dealing with the prejudice pushing against them, all at the same time. It was too much. Ellie felt his mother's eyes disdainfully running over her clothes again. Even if Alfred miraculously recovered, she had no confidence that that he would ever advocate for their relationship outside their very small Grandfield bubble.

It was just another way that Billy had won again. He had lived up to his threat. Ellie made no attempt to follow his trial, outside her obligations of being called as a witness. Nurses spend a lot of time making beds, and Ellie conceded that this was a bed that Billy had made himself. It was time he lay in the mess of his own disturbed choices. She was not going to clean up after him... not this time. He had gone too far.

Work became her refuge, and Ellie dived into her duties as she silently joined the ranks of the war-widows around her neighbourhood. She didn't wear black, yet she grieved as intensely as if she had been Alfred's widow, even though nothing had ever been sealed between them. Others only saw a nurses' uniform and a gentle smile, however there was a black band of mourning tightly constricting her heart. She mourned the 'might-have-beens', the possibilities, the connection, however idealistic and intoxicating and unrealistic it had turned out to be. She mourned the man she had believed him to be. His shadows were much darker than anyone knew. She buried the embarrassment, and the shame, and started singing again... sad laments of a deep loss that had broken her heart. Those around her listened to her mournful songs, as the melodies sadly mirrored the reflection of what every soul felt in a world that had turned in on itself and was dying.

* * *

Part 3

The Cadence of Love

1919

11

Max Whitaker went for a late evening walk around the grounds of Grandfield hospital with his sister, Anna. They paused and sat down on a bench-seat together under a spreading camphor laurel tree. Grandfield Park had been their family home. Anna was fourteen years younger than Max, so they didn't have many memories of their childhood together as brother and sister. Max had climbed these grand old camphor laurel trees as a youngster, but by the time Anna came along, he was immersed in school, captaining cricket teams and football matches and polo events. By the time Anna was old enough to explore climbing trees herself, Max had already left home.

Then war was declared, and the Grandfield house had been taken over by the military to operate as a war hospital. Now it was teeming with wounded, damaged, broken-down soldiers. Without exception, each of these soldiers had left their homeland to fight another man's fight and somehow managed to make that fight their own. Max had done the same thing. The war had not just taken a house away from his family. It had taken his sight. And his ability to speak. Max also lost a leg. Anna had been nursing in another hospital as her way of supporting the war cause. For both of them, the sacrifice didn't feel special, or noble, or altruistic. It just hurt. Now that the war was over, when they paused to calculate what they had lost, they realised many things were a painful reminder of the deficit those losses incurred.

Max never expected that losing the inheritance of Grandfield Park would hurt. For a long time, he had held to the idea that grand old houses which needed staff to manage their unwieldy size and their unwieldy lifestyle, were an outdated idea. Not that he didn't enjoy certain comforts; in fact, he was very much attached to those. He just didn't expect everyone else to pander to his plans and preferences all the time. He could manage that himself.

Once, the only obligation he felt towards this place, was to turn up once a year for the Christmas Gala, put on a jacket and a show, so his life could go on as usual. Business deals and making money was what he was good at. Max had easily occupied the centre of attention back then, and he worked hard and partied hard to preserve his place of influence. But now, as he sat in the evening shadows of the night garden, unable to see the outline of the house in the darkness of his blindness, he realised he loved... not just the brick and the mortar, but the idea of Grandfield being the centre of the community, a hub around which the locals turned. This was not about his personal need to be the centre of attention anymore, but he wanted this house to resume its place as the centre-point of the neighbourhood. Not as some sort of feudal headquarters, but a place where people could shelter under its grand old wings and become strong enough to deal with what their lives brought to them again.

This unexpected pain of losing Grandfield was an albatross around his neck that he had to carry as penance for his blatant disregard of the good fortune that such an inheritance had been. And now, like Coleridge's famous poem, *Ancient Mariner*, Max felt the weight of his dismissal of something that had been good. How that weighed him down! Oh, how he tried to accept the reality that he may never reclaim his legacy or have the opportunity to make it right.

Max sat in the dark of the garden, grateful that very few people knew who he was, and he wanted to keep it that way. His days of being the celebrity in the limelight was over. He stayed in his allocated room at the hospital and only went out at night under the cover of darkness when Anna came to walk with him. He pretty much avoided everyone else. Especially his parents. They lived in the Stablemasters residence, embarrassed and isolated by the humiliation that they occupied servant's quarters. They didn't have anything to do with the hospital, except for his mother's recent insistence on reinstating weekly dances in the Glasshouse, to fundraise for the hospital, supporting the returned servicemen. Good on Mother... doing her part.

Max had avoided the other patients religiously. He didn't need someone recognising a captain in the King's Army, as a broken-down, blind shell. And Max certainly didn't need the community seeing the heir of Grandfield lost at sea, with no wind in his sails to give him momentum or drive. Ancient Mariner indeed. The war had made him grow up, and grow old, and grow humble... and he didn't like any of it.

Every night patients bundled into the Grandfield dining room, which now, instead of being the fancy dining experience it used to be, looked like a military mess hall. Soldiers, missing limbs and missing mates, were going through their routines, trying to make sense of their lives, and what to do next. Max was the same. Being the heir to Grandfield made no difference here. Once, as he was nursed back to life, he had experienced a glimmer of something beautiful in all of that pain. But that was a lifetime ago. As he sat in the shadows of the grand old house that used to be his home, he wondered how life could ever be good again.

Every night, before the patients started to eat their meal, Ellie came to the dining room and sang a song, a hymn, a ditty, or a popular ballad. No one would eat until her rendition was finished, and then Ellie would close her item by saying a prayer – a blessing of Grace over the food and the health of all partakers before they ate. Then she would smile and refuse to give the encore that they always tried to entice from her lips. Max never went to the dining room with the other patients, but he would sit outside with Anna, and listen to Ellie sing, while they drank a cup of soup together. And then then they would walk through the shadows, along the paths of the garden together.

The music of the hymn that Ellie sang tonight resonated through the open window, out into the garden as if they sat in the gallery of a grand concert hall...

> *I come to the garden alone,*
> *While the dew is still on the roses,*
> *And the voice I hear falling on my ear,*
> *The Son of God discloses...*

Max had spent months in this hospital as a patient fighting for his life. Fighting to regain his footing. This garden had been his sanctuary. He had spent many hours treading these paths in the dark hours, escorted by his nurse Mim Hillman. She was the nurse by his side who had brought him back to life, rescued from the brink of death as a cot-case. She coached him to use his balance with a prosthetic leg... to navigate without sight... and to share his heart without a voice. His ability to speak was permanently damaged, so Morse Code become his first language.

As Max recovered from his war-wounds, the driving need to go back to the service, to finish what he had started, would not be silenced. He was only admitted due to the high level of intelligence he had been privy to. But the second deployment was even worse than the first. He needed to navigate military systems without sight, or a voice. Frustration and rage became the other enemy that dogged his every move. It had been like passing through the eye of the storm and then being ripped apart as the cyclone changed direction and ferociously destroyed what had been left with greater savagery than the first time around. The music floated from the dining room and continued to penetrate the chaos, to calm the storm in his soul, and parted the dark, heavy clouds to offer a refreshing shower of life soaking rain.

> *And He walks with me, and He talks with me,*
> *And He tells me I am His own,*
> *And the joy we share as we tarry there,*
> *None other, has ever, known!*

There was something about that song. Something about the idea of the garden. The music rang around his heart. Max knew what it was like to 'tarry' in a garden with someone he loved. But he had never really understood until that moment, that regardless of the people in his life, the life-giving part, the regenerative part came from walking through the garden with the Son of God first.

> *He speaks and the sound of His voice,*
> *Is so sweet the birds hush their singing,*
> *And the melody that he gave to me,*
> *Within my heart is ringing .*

He sat still as the lyrics soaked through his pain. He shuffled over on the bench seat, symbolically making room for the Son of God, for Jesus to come and join him on the bench. And as he moved, something in his heart shifted too. He gasped as he felt the chains which pinned that heavy albatross to his neck, break away and the weight lifted from his shoulders. Internally something else moved, as if all the embedded shrapnel that had torn at his body loosened and left, and the bleeding stopped. The internal rage, shifted and separated like storm clouds parting. He wasn't sure if it was really a physical thing that happened, but he tangibly felt hope sear though him, cauterising the wounds on his soul. There was more healing to come, he was certain of that, but there was a deep awareness that God had always been there, breathing life into his wounded body bringing him back from the brink of death, and God would not leave him now in this broken-down shell; God would continue his healing until it was complete.

Again, Max felt that realisation reinforced in his heart. It was unfair to put the responsibility of this healing onto other people – even people he truly loved, when they were bleeding themselves. This gift of wholeness was the domain of the divine. He'd heard people say their soulmate 'completed' them, 'sustained' them, 'fulfilled' them. He'd even had hoped for that himself. But it was not fair to attribute that role to any person; it was too heavy for them to carry. The clarity Max felt in that moment was like sight had been restored. Even in the blackness, he was no longer groping around in the dark; now he had an anchor to pivot towards the people he loved. It was the same profound strength he felt as Mim read her Bible to him, infusing him with the determination to do what he needed to do to be strong again. He knew what it was like not to have a future, and in that moment, he humbly realised that his future had been restored and given back to him.

When Max had first been fitted with his 'limb', he bucked hard and hadn't wanted to accept what it meant, until he realised it was a reason to get out of the room, and to go walking with Mim. How he loved those walks every night with Mim. Those garden walks under the cover of darkness, had been the lightest, most beautiful conversations that he had ever experienced. And then another piece clicked into place. As Mim read her mother's Bible to him, his heart connected with God with a depth of honesty he hadn't known before. Months and months of grace-filled pages watered his cracked and brittle heart while she cared for him. But when he left, he had no one to read to him, and the rhythm of this practice of prayer was absorbed by the rigid routines of the army. And slowly his heart had crusted over again.

There were a few things Max was certain of as he sat in the garden listening to Ellie sing her evening number. Yes, there was no doubt that Ellie could really sing. Another certainty was that his sister, Anna, breathed light into everything with her warmth and her sparkle. And... the largest truth of all... the one that he could no longer deny, was that he was still in love with Mim. Yes, he was. Still

Mim was not just a nurse who saved his life; she had brought him back to life and taught him how to live again. He had insisted she learn Morse Code, so they could talk together. She was quick at learning, quick to laugh and quick to challenge him. And back then he was convinced there was a mutual connection. But he didn't know whether his affection for her was enduring, or just a fantasy that had grown larger than life over the years since they parted. He had to allow that he was probably not the first patient to attached themselves to a beautiful woman who had nursed them back to life. It could have just been part of her job... a professional obligation. In these days, when everything was so uncertain, a few years was a lifetime. Who knew how affections might change in a world that was trying to catch its breath after being smothered by the horror of a worldwide war? Still, Max was clear on another certainty: he needed to find out for sure. He needed to know if Mim even remembered him, or if she had moved on unhindered by the memory of the months she looked after him. Or the other possibility was the grand hope that she did remember, and she was open to the idea of being together.

When Max was wounded, he had been sent to Grandfield to recover. The army was less interested in preserving his life, and more concerned in protecting the wartime secrets that the expertise of his team had uncovered. Grandfield was a small, inconsequential rehabilitation facility where no one would go looking for war intelligence. To protect the intelligence, no one on staff had been given his name, just a file number. His supervising army officer, the staff doctor and Mim – his allocated nurse, were the only ones who knew he was admitted as a patient there. He found out that the staff doctor had been physically assaulted and retired on medical grounds. This meant that, even if Mim wanted to, she had no way to contact him. This was up to him. One point reassured him – Mim had once been Anna's governess... so this was his starting place. He had to find Mim. And Anna would help him.

As the music of Ellie's song faded into the sounds of the evening, Max contracted with himself to be strict about resuming his communion with the Writer of the Words that Mim had read to him from her Bible every morning.

> *And the joy we share as we tarry there,*
> *None other, has ever, known!*

He tapped the lyrics with his cane as he sat there immersed in his thoughts as the music rang through his heart, long after the song had passed. And he paused, a frown puckering his brow, as he thought he heard an echo through the dark, of dashes and dots... singing the song along with him in Morse. He tapped again, and it echoed back. He reached out to Anna who was sitting beside him. She squeezed his hand affectionately, but sat quietly, immersed in her own thoughts. She had not noticed the rapping... so perhaps he imagined it.

He tapped again. Perhaps his quest would be solved quickly if Mim was still working at the hospital. Again, he heard the tapping echo through the dark.

"WHO ARE YOU" he tapped.

"PRIVATE PHILIP SINCLAIR SIR"

Oh. His heart sank. Not Mim. "COME HERE" he tapped.

"YES CAPTAIN" Philip emerged from the shadows and stood at attention before the bench seat. "I AM HERE SIR" he tapped very apologetically with the stick in his hand.

"AT EASE" Max tapped. "I CAN HEAR YOU / I CANT SPEAK BUT YOU CAN TALK TO ME" Max noticed an idea forming in his mind.

"Sorry Sir," Philip said, and then turned and acknowledged Anna with a nod. "Evening Ma'am."

Anna opened her eyes wide and nodded in return. She sat still and silent, amazed that Max was engaging with someone who obviously had been a soldier. Since Max returned home, he had avoided all military personnel like the plague. She wasn't about to interrupt.

The man still stood at attention. "I am very sorry to disturb you both Sir, but I haven't seen you around the garden for a while. First saw you a few years ago when I was a patient here myself."

"MY ADMISSION WAS SUPPOSED TO BE COVERT / APPARENTLY NOTHING GETS PAST YOU STILL"

"Thank you, Sir. Although no one believed me at the time. Thought I was crazy. Guess that kept your cover after all."

"ARE YOU A PATIENT HERE SOLDIER"

"Oh no, Captain. I was discharged from the hospital and the army a while ago, but I still come here every night to the garden to listen to Ellie sing. I just live down the road. I mean no harm. Ellie and me, we grew up together around these parts. Sir, I think Ellie's voice is the most beautiful thing. It reminds me of a better time." He didn't pause to consider how the bullying he grew up with could be thought of as better than this.

"I SEE" then Max smiled and shook his head. "IN A MANNER OF SPEAKING". When was the last time Max felt comfortable enough to make a joke about his limitation. "DO YOU HAVE A JOB PRIVATE".

"No Captain. Just fixing up my mother's house, while looking for options, Sir. Not a lot of call for a Sapper around these parts... even a first-class signaller... not now anyways... and the usual labouring jobs, well, there are always a lot of better applicants." He shuffled his feet and cleared his throat.

"COME TO THE HOSPITAL TOMORROW 0800 / ROOM 7".

"Yes Sir!"

"WEAR A SUIT".

"Yes Sir!"

* * *

Flip lived alone in his mother's house. She had passed away not long after he was discharged from hospital. His one consolation was that he was there to look after her in those last weeks. She had been so proud of him. It was another one of those things that didn't seem right. Fighting another's man's fight meant he couldn't stay home and fight for the one who had always been there for him. He really believed that if he had been home during those war years, his

Mum would still be alive. She was another casualty of this Great War. One that would never be recognised, no plaques or memorials raised in her name. This was her sacrifice of service as well.

Philip stood outside the door of Room 7. He adjusted his tortoiseshell-framed glasses, pulled at his tie and smoothed down his sleeves. He didn't have a suit of his own, so he had gone to visit his Uncle Seb who was much older than his Mum. He had given him this suit and a tie. It was a navy pinstriped suit, old fashioned in its style and since Seb was a tall man, it didn't fit very well. But Philip had rummaged through his mother's sewing box and sown up the sleeves and hemmed the trouser legs. He had used his mother's old box clothes-iron to press military creases along the legs, and he polished his boots with meticulous care. He swallowed hard and knocked at the door.

He heard the rapping of Captain Whitaker's cane. "COME IN".

Philip opened the door.

"ON TIME / THAT IS ENCOURAGING SOLDIER". Max tapped his approval with a smile. "TAKE A SEAT".

"Yes Captain."

He paused and nodded. "PHILIP WE NEED TO SET SOME NEW RULES / I AM NOT YOUR CAPTAIN ANYMORE / YOU ARE NOT IN THE ARMY / CALL ME MAX / AT THE VERY LEAST MR WHITAKER"

"Yes Capt... Mr Whitaker, Sir."

"PHILIP I WANT TO OFFER YOU A JOB / I NEED
SOMEONE WHO KNOWS MORSE / YOU ARE THE BEST"

"Thank you, Sir."

"I NEED A PERSONAL ASSISTANT / SOMEONE TO
MANAGE MY DIARY / INTERPRET DURING MEETINGS
/ READ CORRESPONDENCE TO ME / WRITE LETTERS /
THAT SORT OF THING"

"Yes Sir!"

"I AM OFFERING THIS JOB TO YOU / IT IS NOT AN
ORDER / THIS IS YOUR CHOICE"

"Yes Capt... Sir. I understand Sir."

"SO PHILIP DO YOU WANT THE JOB"

"Very much Sir. I want to work with you again Sir."

"THAT IS GOOD NEWS"

"It is Sir. I am grateful for the opportunity. Like I said, not a
lot of openings for a Sapper now-a-days. If I'd been an engineer, it
might be different... but communications... not so much."

"ONE OTHER THING"

"Yes Sir?"

"WHAT HAPPENED BEFORE / OUT ON THE FIELD
/ THAT DOESNT COME HERE / WE START FRESH"

"But Sir...

"I MEAN IT / I NEED YOUR SKILL AS A
SIGNALMAN AND CRYPTOGRAPHER / I EMPLOY ON
THIS BASIS"

"Yes, Mr Whitaker, Sir."

"CAN YOU START STRAIGHT AWAY"

"Yes Sir!"

That was step number one. He had hired eyes and a tongue who could see and talk for him; an intelligent man who would read between the lines, honest and loyal. Max had hardly slept. His mind was flooding with new ideas and strategies. He hadn't told his parents he was back home, but now he needed to meet with his father, and work out an approach to reinstate the Whitaker custodianship over this property. It needed to be done in such a way as to protect the running of the hospital for returned service men and women going forward. To support the healing of this generation was the best legacy he could pass on.

* * *

12

"Excuse me Nurse?"

Ellie closed the cabinet that held bottles of potions and elixirs and locked the door. She put the key in her pocket and turned around. "Yes, how can I help you?"

A man in an awkward fitting navy-blue pinstripe suit was standing there with a clipboard and he shuffled his feet. He stared at Ellie through his glasses and swallowed hard.

"Sir, are you okay?"

He said nothing and swallowed, clearing his throat.

"Flip?" She stared and shook her head. "I mean... Mr Sinclair? Is that you? It is Ellie Pollard... do you remember me?" He had been so confused and unsettled when he was a patient.

He barely nodded.

"Mr Sinclair, what are you doing here?"

"I..." He coughed and swallowed. "I... I need to talk to..." His voice trailed off and he looked away. Ellie was as pretty as ever. And kind. Even the way she spoke was as melodic as her singing, like music. He coughed. He wished he could just pick up where their friendship had left off. But she was the Sister-in-Charge of a whole rehabilitation facility. She was Ellie Pollard. She was someone. He was not.

"Are you here to visit anyone in particular?"

"Yes. No. No, not really. Not a visit. Not a patient." He blinked awkwardly.

"Oh. Well then, what is it that you need?"

"Umm..." His tongue-tie tightened to constrict his whole body.

Ellie looked at the watch pinned to her uniform. She reached out her hand and led him over to a chair and sat him down. She felt him tremble. "Mr Sinclair... Philip – may I call you Philip?"

He nodded mutely.

"Philip, I want you to take a breath. Like we used to. Can you do that?"

He nodded mutely... and breathed. Slowly. Slowly. In and out.

"So, you are here to visit someone?"

He nodded.

"And this person... you said was not a patient?"

He nodded.

"Oh. Are you here to visit me?'

He gasped and shook his head vigorously. "Oh, No! No..." He would never presume.

Ellie grinned. "Well, that's a shame... but I am not offended. May I ask, why you are here?" She passed him a glass of water.

He nodded and closed his eyes. Miss Lambert always started her singing exercises with a glass of water: "Hmm–Hmm–Ahhh!" Those exercises helped his childhood asthma. "Hmm–Hmm–Ahhh!"

This very odd prescription which the family doctor gave his mother had made such a difference. Every week he went early to help Miss Lambert set out the chairs instead of paying the choir fee to cover music books. He was included in the lessons for his effort, but the greatest benefit for him was that he also got to see Ellie under the cover of a singing group. It was strange to think that joining the community choir, also made it possible for him to join the army. He took another sip. "Hmm–Hmm–Ahhh!"

"See! There you have it. Feeling better?"

He nodded. "I am here for work. For Mr Whitaker."

"Mr Whitaker? As in the *Grandfield* Whitakers? You work for him?"

He nodded and shook his head as if clearing the fog. He took another deep breath and sat up straighter as if his strength was returning. He put down the glass. "I need to speak with Sister Hillman. Sister Mim Hillman. Is she here?"

"Oh. Well, that is easy request to help with; she is in Room Four... just there on the right." She raised her brow and wondered why he would need to speak with Min. "You are fortunate to catch her... she normally works nights but she is covering for someone for a couple of weeks."

He stood up. Room Four had been his room. Weeks and weeks of delirium and confusion with Ellie's voice floating in and out of his awareness. Ellie's voice.

"Philip – are you okay? Do you need me to come with you?"

"No. No. This is okay. It is just a message. Mr Whitaker said all I have to do is to deliver the message... like the army. It is not my responsibility how she responds. I should be used to enemy fire," he said with a trace of a grin.

"Well, I know you are good at what you do. Like you said, delivering messages is not new. You can do this."

"Yes. Yes, I can." He stood up, squared his shoulders, and adjusted the lapels on his pinstriped jacket.

"Thank you, Ellie... Nurse ... ahh, Sister Pollard... you are very kind."

Ellie watched him walk to Room Four as if he was plunging into a battle zone.

"Sister Hillman?"

Mim looked up from the bed she was making. "Yes?" She stared at the man in the pinstriped suit and pursed her lips. "Oh. It's you."

"Yes Ma'am." Philip shuffled uncomfortably and clung to his clipboard.

"Well? What is it that you want?"

"Ma'am, Capt... Mr Whitaker wanted me to tell you that he requires you come to his office to see him." He tried to make it sound as harmless a request as he could. Ever since the New Year's Dance Captain Whitaker was obsessed with reconnecting with Miss Hillman. He didn't really understand why. She was very abrasive.

The nurse stood up tall. "He *requires* it? Does he now?'

"Yes, Ma'am." He looked away and stepped back.

"Well, you can tell *Mister* Whitaker that the hospital administrator and the nursing staff have no bearing on each other. I am not required to meet with him, and he cannot summon me."

Oh, that was not good. Philip stared at her in horror. Who would say 'No' to Captain Whitaker? "Oh Ma'am, please. Please just come."

"No! I have no obligation at all to attend his office. My job is here with the patients."

"But..."

"No."

Philip reminded himself again what the captain had said. *Just deliver the message.* "Very well Ma'am. If you change your mind Mr Whitaker will see you at any time."

"Don't disturb yourself. I won't."

Philip left, and as he passed by the Nurses' desk, Sister Pollard nodded to him, her eyes large behind her spectacles. "How did you go?"

He shook his head. But then a hint of smile leaked through the anxiety of his failure. "It does mean I will have to come back tomorrow. And perhaps the next day... until she relents. If she does at all."

Ellie grinned. "Well then Mr Sinclair, I will see you tomorrow. It is your obligation to be thorough in delivering your messages." She said that with a wink.

His eyes looked startled behind his eyeglasses, and he quickly left down the stairs as if escaping a fire.

* * *

The next day, Ellie watched the corridors to see if Philip would come to the ward again as he said. At zero-nine-thirty hours, Philip appeared at the nurses' desk with his clipboard in hand. "Good morning, Ellie... Oh... I'm sorry... I mean Sister... Sister Pollard." He cleared his throat and stood straight at attention. "Sister Pollard, I was wondering if I could see Nurse... Sister Hillman." Why did he keep forgetting that hospitals had their own rank and file? In the army it was constantly in your face. This new arrangement was confusing. Captain Whitaker was his boss, and yet he insisted that rank and file didn't apply anymore. Flip needed this job, and he didn't want to overstep his role.

Ellie twisted her lips thoughtfully. "Hmm. I think Sister Hillman is actually very busy just now." She pointed to a chair. "Would you like a cup of tea while you wait Philip?"

"Tea? Here? Now?"

"We are making tea from the trolley for the patients. If you are inclined..."

"Oh. Well. Yes. I guess. If she is very busy."

"She is. Unquestionably run off her feet. Would you like milk? We have a house-cow. Well, it is a *hospital*-cow, I guess. Because this is a small hospital, on larger grounds... there are all sorts of privileges that we are indulged with... like fresh milk...even in the city."

He smiled at that. A few years ago, deep under enemy fire, a simple glass of milk, with a slice of bread and butter would have been the ultimate luxury. It honed back his appreciation of essentials to the barest of basics. "A drop of milk would be amazing. Don't leave your patients short though."

"That is thoughtful of you Mr Sinclair," she said officially as she stirred through the milk and handed him the cup. The tea-lady came and whisked the trolley away to do the rounds through the ward. Ellie sat down on the chair by her desk and flicked randomly through some charts. "Are you enjoying your job, Mr Sinclair?" she asked after some time.

Philip set his cup down on the corner of the desk. "I feel very fortunate to have this position. The Hospital's Administrator's Personal Assistant. That is what my paperwork says. In reality, it is just what I was doing in the army: anything the captain requires... but with much less noise, and much, much less danger."

"Oh, I don't know," said Ellie with a grin. "You are here on a dangerous mission. It seems could suffer a great deal of enemy fire from Sister Hillman." Ellie paused. "I don't think she likes your Boss," she added quietly with a twinkle in her eye.

"I don't know why; Captain Whitaker's unit was the best to be assigned to. When I enlisted, we were told signallers had the cushy job, being in communications... but actually, the reverse is true. At one point, the life expectancy for a Sapper on duty was three days. It is a miracle I am here."

"I'm glad you are part of the miracle," said Ellie warmly.

"Dealing with landmines was part of the job. Captain Whitaker saved my life... but he was injured doing it. I don't mind telling people that. Some reckon that he is a bit lofty, you know, since he came from money... but he worked jolly hard, and he didn't mind getting his boots muddy. He went under fire just like the rest of us. That's what I remember. It made a huge difference."

"Is that why you got the job here, since you fought together... you know, being brothers-in-arms?"

"I guess it looks like nepotism, but... well, Captain... I mean *Mister* Whitaker... you know he really wants me to drop the captain, but I find it so hard, and it seems disrespectful." He took a drink from his cup and shrugged in a disarming way. "He tells me I got the job because I'm a first-class signaller. Quick. He needs quick."

"What sort of signals do you use?"

"All sorts... but the captain uses Morse Code the most. A lot. You know... since he lost his voice and sight."

"Then it is good that he has you."

"You may think that Ellie, but the reverse is true. It is good that I can help him. He tells me my work makes a huge difference, and that it has nothing to do with owing him anything... but the reality is, I owe him my life." He stood to his feet. "Guess it is time to face the music. Thank you for the cup of tea. That was a bonus I was not expecting this morning. Especially the conversation that went with it." He stopped after a couple of steps. "Sister Hillman wasn't really that busy just now, was she?"

"We are always very busy on this ward, Mr Sinclair," Ellie said with that adorable twinkle.

Philip nodded and smiled. He turned and walked to the door of Room Two, which Ellie had indicated and returned in a matter of seconds on his way out. "I will see you tomorrow," he said quietly with a nod and a smile, and he filled out his suit just a little more.

* * *

Each morning Philip arrived at the ward at zero-nine-thirty hours. There was always the hope that another cup of tea might be offered. He would hover for a moment before alighting on the chair like a restless dragonfly, while Ellie poured his cup of tea and added milk.

"Mr Sinclair, I was thinking about how you said you were a signaller. How did you know you were good at it when you had never done anything like that before?"

"Well, I guess they took one look at me and realised that I couldn't hold a candle to most of the normal recruits. My asthma means I don't have the stamina the others have. I'm pretty sure that without a war, I would not have passed muster, but they lowered the bar some and let people through. The doctor who did my medical told me I was one of those people. He recommended more support duties. We never had the money for me to go to university, so I self-taught myself morse even before the war broke out, and my aptitude test identified I'm good with numbers and patterns. That's mostly what a cryptographer is... identifying and deciphering patterns... so they shipped me down to do the basic signaller's course. They sent me over to the more advanced training because it came kind of natural for me. It was all very condensed because of the war, but it wasn't long before I passed the syllabus for being a first-class signaller. I was drafted into Captain Whitaker's troop straight away. It was pretty intense, but it actually felt good, knowing I could do

something to help. Some used to scoff and call us the Lyrebird Corp
– you know, since a lyrebird has no song of their own. Sappers are
the combat engineers, and their support is considered well... but the
communications branch is there to mimic what we are told, and to
listen in on other's messages... secure them, translate them. Didn't
bother me none... what they said about the sappy lyrebird. As a kid I
was pretty used to insults. And this was important: we had some
pretty strange stuff come through, especially those last couple of days
we came under fire...”

Every day Philip spoke about some aspect of his life as a
signaller. Now that the war was over, the secrecy applied to his
mission no longer seemed relevant. It felt good to talk about those
salient, silent years as a sappy lyrebird. Ellie was the only person who
had ever asked or had ever listened.

Ellie found it refreshing the way Philip trusted her with his
story. Most of the soldiers who came through these wards refused to
talk about anything connected to their experience during the war and
what had happened. Their silence was a black mould that ate at their
soul.

* * *

Philip handed Ellie a little box as she passed him his cup of tea. She lifted the lid and curiously looked inside. She drew out a small piece of sheet music folded into the shape of a bird. "Oh Flip! Look at this. It is beautiful! So cute."

"It is a little songbird. Our Unit was made up of a mix of allied servicemen. We had a Japanese cryptographer join us. Strange little man, but really clever. No one could pronounce his real name, so we all called him Fuji. The others weren't so keen on him since he was quiet and mostly kept to himself. But the Japanese have been important allies in this war, and he became a good mate. He was always teaching me another paper figure to fold. They call it the Art of Origami. He said it was good practice for working patterns. Some of them were simple, and I'd remember them pretty quick, but others were very complicated. But this little songbird... this was my favourite. I made a lot of them. It reminded me of you."

"Me?" Ellie propped the little bird on her desk. "Well, this little bird can sit here and remind me not to forget to sing. Thank you Philip."

"Sister Pollard, I don't mean to be an Indian giver, but I was wondering if I could have that little box back?"

She smiled and passed over the box. She had been intending to put paperclips in it. "Of course, Philip. Thank you. I love the little bird."

The next morning, Philip held out the box again. "Can I trade for a cup of tea?"

She looked at the box and then met his eyes seriously with a pause. "No. Absolutely, you cannot." His eyes went wide, and he retracted his hand with a stammer. Ellie went to the tea cart and picked up the large teapot in its woollen cosy. "The cup of tea is free, and if you have something for me, you can offer it, but without any trade. That way, nothing is owed. Just friends being friends."

Huh. Mr Whitaker had said that too. *Nothing is owed.* "Oh. Okay...". He sat down. He didn't even notice that he no longer waited for permission. "Well, I do enjoy my morning cup of tea, and I did want to give you this...". He passed over the box and noticed that her fingers touched his as she took it from his hand. "Friends being friends."

Ellie opened the lid, and lifted out another paper bird, made from sheet music, this one with its wings outstretched. Her serious face melted into a glorious smile as she admired its craftmanship, and she propped it up beside the other.

After he had finished his cup, Philip stood up and paused. "Ellie, do you think Sister Hillman will ever come and see Mr

Whitaker? I don't feel I'm doing a good job when she shuts me down like this."

"I think Mr Whitaker is right: you can't make her go. This is not the army anymore." It felt liberating to say that. It also felt decent that Philip was not strong-arming his way around. They had patients who still expected their military rank-and-file to grant them privileges. "But I tell you what, I might have a word with her... to see if I can't exert a little encouragement in that direction."

"Thank you, Ellie. I'd appreciate that. Mr Whitaker always looks so hopeful when I go back, and I hate that I have to tell him over and over that she's not coming."

"You know Philip. I think you are a very considerate man. It is refreshing to see how much you care about your job."

"Ellie, I don't think I care about my job that much at all. But people... that is different. I *do* care about them. And if I care for people, I will do my job well. I can see what this means to Mr Whitaker." And he tucked his empty little box under his arm, went and found Sister Hillman, and delivered his message. Ellie looked after his retreating figure thoughtfully as he left the ward to return to his desk outside Mr Whitakers office.

* * *

"Mim? Can I have a word?" Ellie sat down beside her as she was writing up her charts.

"Yes Sister." Mim closed the chart in front of her.

"Sister? Mim... come on. What's going on? I have never seen the calm, unflappable Mim Hillman in such a mess. You are terse and abrupt. It is not like you. Is there something I can do?"

"I doubt it. My work has not suffered. And my patients are fine."

"You know there has never been an issue with the way you care for your patients."

Mim cleared her throat. "Well, actually, there is something you could do for me."

"Sure... whatever you feel might help."

"Tell that pinstripe-suit guy to stop coming to the ward every morning. He is harassing me."

"Flip... Philip Sinclair? Harassing you?" Ellie laughed. "You can't be serious. You puff in his direction, and he almost falls over. I'm not going to put an embargo on the Hospital's administrator's personal assistant."

"Well, if you won't do that, there is nothing more to be said."

"Why don't you just go to his office and hear the man out?"

"Really? Ellie, we have been friends for a long time, but this... this is none of your business. My work is okay. I am okay. Leave it alone."

"Well, if you won't hear me as your friend, I speak as your supervising Ward Sister. And my observation is that you are not okay. Whatever Max Whitaker needs to talk to you about, is obviously important. To both of you. I suggest you do whatever you need to sort it out. Otherwise, you are going to find yourself in a heap in a corner somewhere, and we will need to look after you. In purely practical terms, I cannot afford to lose my best staff member. Just think about it."

* * *

Ellie was riffling through her desk drawer and then tipped out the wastepaper basket, going through the discarded papers. She looked harassed and disappointed. Every couple of days, even long after Mim had relented and had gone to meet with Max Whitaker, Philip had come to the ward for a cup of tea with her, gifting her with another beautiful paper songbird. She heard someone behind her, and she said rather quickly, "Has anyone seen where my paper birds have gone? I don't want Flip coming and finding them missing."

"Missing?"

She stood up and there was Philip in his too large pinstripe suit looking at her curiously. "Oh Philip, I am so sorry. Perhaps the cleaner threw them out. I loved each one so much and I really, really should have taken them back to my room before this. I am so sorry, but they are gone. They are all gone."

He sat down undisturbed. "Am I too late for a cup of tea?"

"No. I... I just don't understand where they could've gone. Who would have done this? I've been looking for them all morning."

121

Tears pooled on her lashes as she poured a cup and stirred in some extra milk. "I'm so sorry! I am really disappointed they are gone."

"Oh."

"Oh? I thought you would be disappointed as well. All that work and care... it has just disappeared!

"Well... I could make them again. Except the pages of music would be different of course."

"No one has ever taken time to make something like that for me before. Each one was so unique, so special..." Ellie frowned and swiped at her forehead, flustered. She had put so much weight on this act of friendship, but perhaps it had not meant as much to Flip after all. She just thought... that if he had gone to so much trouble... it had meant something to him as well.

Philip stood up in a moment. "Oh Ellie, I'm sorry. I didn't know that this would cause you so much distress..."

"No, I wasn't complaining... I just..." She sat down and shook her head. She was enjoying that she didn't have to hide their friendship behind a uniform now. Flip was still as timid and as courageous as ever. Silent in his own version of strong.

"What I mean is... this..." and he handed over a rather battered hatbox. Ellie raised her brow and noticed that he wasn't carrying his clipboard today.

She swiped at her eyes, took a breath and then placed the box on her knee. She opened the lid to a tangle of cotton thread, sticks and her paper songbirds. Every one of her beloved birds were accounted for as she stared into the box. "You took them? I've been looking for them all morning."

"Dust gatherers, and clutter if they are just sitting on your desk. There were getting to be too many. But I thought by putting them together in this mobile your birds can always fly and sing... all day, every day. That is what they were destined for."

She lifted out the sticks, and the birds fell into a perfectly balanced spiral formation. A thread strung each little body to the twigs, wings outstretched. "Oh Flip, this is beautiful!"

"I thought you might think they would be getting in your way..."

"Oh! This is so wonderful!" She laughed, relief infusing her. She gently put it back in the box and placed it on a chair; then bounced up and gave him a hug. Philip stood there, stiff and awkward. She stepped back as he cleared his throat.

"Philip, are you okay? I'm sorry if..." Her voice trailed off.

"Would you like some help to hang it up? I was thinking in the hallway where it might get a gentle breeze. There is already a hook."

"Huh. Look at that. I have never noticed." Ellie held the ladder while Philip hung the mobile and carefully untangled each thread, so each bird floated freely in the breeze from an open window. He climbed down and they admired it together. "It looks good there," she said. "Just perfect."

"Ellie, would you walk with me around the garden some time, after your shift maybe?" He said it quickly and looked away. "I know that is something you used to do after your shift."

"Oh. I haven't done that for a long time. Not since..."

"Oh. I understand..."

"But Philip, if you were with me, I think I would like to try that again," she replied without moving.

"Really?"

"Yes. Really. You are my best friend after all. Remember? We promised. I finish at three-thirty... probably won't get away until four though."

"Oh." Now he understood more. Friends being friends. He'd heard of those who were relegated to the friend zone, left standing there while the one they loved moved on with someone else. "Today?" Well, he would take what he was offered.

"Yes, today. I look forward to it." Ellie watched his shoulders sag, and he seemed to walk away defeated. She didn't understand. She had said 'yes'. Well, it was a start. Finally, she was going walking with Flip Sinclair. Ellie could not bring herself to go walking after she found Alfred's shattered spectacles in the garden. But this time she rationalised that there would be other people around in the afternoon. She was sure that if she was with Flip she would feel safe.

They walked around the path, quickly and efficiently, just as if Ellie was still on the ward. Philip kept pace, checking at every lap that she was okay. He seemed to understand that this was more than just walking along a path for her. He experienced that same sort of feeling himself. Sometimes it felt like he was back in the trenches, and he could never tell when that feeling would hit.

Slowly Ellie started to relax her pace. "You know Philip, I have never had such a unique gift made just for me. Those birds are such a special thing that you did."

"I'm glad that you like them," he said warmly. Then he glanced at her curiously. "But I remember Billy giving you all sorts of flash things. I could never compete with that."

"The difference being... this is a gift that tells me you were thinking about me, and it was not about making yourself look good. You obviously don't realise that Billy stole most of the things he gave me. I always tried to give them back to their owner. The ones I couldn't locate I passed on anonymously to the police. I think Constable Trey knew it was me because he would always ask if I was okay when he saw me at the market." He'd tell me Billy was not a good friend for me, and I could do better. Billy never knew that when I would get him to tell me the story behind what he gave me, it was so I could work out who the owner was. He liked talking about himself, so it wasn't too hard. Problem is... I think it encouraged him more, so in the end my data gathering proved counterproductive."

Philip spoke seriously. "Be reassured: I didn't pilfer the hymnal from the church to make your birds. I went to a second-hand bookstore and legitimately purchased a copy. I have the receipt if you want to check."

"Of course, I am not going to check. I trust you, Philip. I always have."

"I tried to match the hymn with the bird."

"Each day when you gave me a bird, I sang that hymn at dinnertime."

"I know. It felt like a thank you... you singing those songs."

"It felt like you were choosing the songs for me."

"Perhaps I was. The first little songbird I made is from the music of the hymn, *In the Garden*. That one is my favourite." This was the song that brought them together again.

"Mine too. Mine too...". And Ellie linked her arm in his elbow a little tighter as they walked in the garden together. It would not be long before she needed to go to the dining room. Tonight, she determined, as she floated towards the hall, she would sing a popular song. Something upbeat and happy. It felt like she was finally able to start feathering her nest in real life.

* * *

14

The afternoon shadows elongated, and the birds were settling in the trees for the night. Philip was sitting on a bench in the garden. "Thank you for meeting me here, Ellie," he said. He was agitated and unsettled. He restlessly stood to his feet as she walked over to him. "Do you mind if we walk?"

"Not at all. Is everything okay?"

"Well... I think so... maybe... no. I have to confess that I have a problem. I honestly don't know what to do about it."

Her eyes lit with concern. His face was creased in anxiety; his step was short and hurried. "Is it your health? Work?" When he shook his head, Ellie reached out and took his hand. "I am no good at guessing games Philip; you are going to have to tell me."

"It is..." He swallowed and stared at her holding his hand. "It is Mrs Whitaker. The captain's mother."

"Oh. *Mrs* Whitaker. What about *her*?" Ellie had very little to do with the Grandfield matriarch. On purpose. Mrs Whitaker had wanted Ellie to sing at a charity concert more than once. But the first time Ellie was asked, it didn't line up with her work roster, and she couldn't get the shifts off. Mrs Whitaker thought that was hardly a sufficient reason to decline her demands and was outright rude about it. Ellie was not too surprised: like Mother, like daughter. She remembered how Anna was. After that, Ellie just made sure she was working whenever another concert came around. Mrs Whitaker was on about it again for the Christmas Gala and New Year's Party. Ellie just said that as the supervising Sister, it was her responsibility to work, so she could release her other staff to attend.

Philip swallowed again and pulled his hand away. Ellie was everything to him, and she deserved so much more than being tangled in his mess. "It is okay, I will work it out."

"Philip? No. Flip. Flip!" She stopped walking and reached out to pull him around to face her. "Listen to me Flip. Friends forever remember. Friends are supposed to help each other."

He looked at her uncertain. "You called me Flip."

"I'm sorry. I can't get used to the whole Philip, Mr Sinclair thing. We are not at work now, and you're not my patient. You are my friend Flip! You always have been, so I am just going to call you that. Your friendship has been a constant for me in uncertain times. I have needed that."

"Me? Constant? But I am so messed up. There are always other confident, tough, strong people around you... like Doctor Redmond." Just one of many who wanted to take Ellie out.

Ahh. Ellie glanced away. As always, he was retreating again. She had to take this slowly... gently. Ellie shrugged nonchalantly and took his arm as they resumed walking. "Well, in case you haven't noticed, Dr Redmond is not here, and I have been walking with you Flip Sinclair, for a while now. No one else."

Of course he noticed. But he didn't think that it meant anything to her, at least not like Doctor Redmond. She used to look at him differently. Very differently. "Ellie, did you ever find out what happened to Doctor Redmond... after... you know..."

"Well, he was unconscious when he left here. He did eventually come out of the coma, and he is now being nursed at home. Still not very independent, as far as I know." Imposed upon by a matriarchal regime that dominated his life.

"So, you follow his progress." It was an observation, more than a question.

"I did for a while... knew one of his nurses."

"Didn't you want to look after him yourself?" It was something he couldn't understand. It seemed to go against Ellie's nature, that she would abandon someone she cared about. And she really had cared for him. He knew because she had that look.

"You know me well Flip. At the time I would have walked over live coals for him. But his family didn't want me around. I smelt too strongly of 'common'. And also... apparently, he was already engaged to someone else."

"Oh Ellie. I am so sorry. I didn't know that."

"Well, neither did I... until after he was admitted to the hospital. I haven't actually published this information since it's all a bit humiliating. But as they say... I missed that train for a reason. It also means that since then, I have not been too inclined to go out with anyone, so it is good to be here with you. Besides, I like your sort of strong Flip. You told me once you noticed some of strong things in me. I never forgot that. They inspired me to keep going. I see those things in you too."

"What things?" Surely Ellie was being polite.

"It seems that so much about your world is terrifying... and yet you keep showing up. That takes courage. You keep giving it a shot. And doing it well, I might add."

Flip shook his head. "Really? I... there's no denying I am..." His voice trailed off. He expected the real hero wouldn't find the world 'terrifying' or difficult. He knew Ellie deserved someone great, someone who didn't struggle. He knew she would be better off without him but he couldn't bring himself to leave her alone. Not when she would smile and invite him to walk with her. He just couldn't. Coward.

Ellie shrugged matter-of-factly. "Well, you can't get rid of me. We promised we would always be friends." She grabbed his hand. "Remember?" And she twisted her hold into that awkward secret handshake.

Flip swallowed. She was right. He had promised. It was a promised he had to keep. Friends forever, even if some other handsome, robust, composed, remarkable doctor came along again. It was the first time he could actually relate to Billy's maniacal jealousy. He thought about those times when he was an in-patient, scurrying through the garden at night, pretending to look for Captain Whitaker. Sure, that was part of it, but mostly he just needed to be sure this doctor was doing right by her. If the Doctor got too close, he would do some crazy thing, and she would take him back to the ward. He would always be Ellie's friend, even if that meant stepping aside when she wanted to go walking with some other clever doctor. Just now, Flip thought that if he went walking with her, even while she just wanted to be friends, it gave him the space to keep others at bay. He imagined that at some point, someone else would come in and barrel him to the ground for walking with Ellie again. It was probably inevitable, but he would do it anyway. He felt his life was always destined to be pummelled and dunked in the water trough... while some other bad-mannered kid got to walk Ellie Pollard down the street. He took a breath. He loved her enough to do it anyway. He couldn't help that.

Ellie smiled reassuringly. "So, are you going to tell me? I know Mrs Whitaker is difficult to manage. If there is something she has said or demanded of you... it might be easier to solve the problem by putting our heads together and working on it with each other."

"How did you know she said something?"

"Mrs Whitaker is not known for being either subtle or sensitive. Actually, I have personally found she can be quite demanding and rude."

Flip chuckled. "Wow! I think, Ellie Pollard, that is the harshest thing I have ever heard you say. Harsh... but true."

There. How Ellie watched for those moments. Those moments when Flip relaxed enough for the echoes of the shy, sensible Flip she knew as a kid to seep through... the one who joked with her when they were alone and no one else was around. Now he was always vigilant. Always on guard. Always alert. She smiled gently again. "And you thought I was perfect. See I have my own version of mess as well."

His eyes smiled and he shook his head. He was still pretty sure Ellie was perfect. "Okay." He took a breath and braced himself. "This is embarrassing. Mrs Whitaker said that since I am around the Whitakers a lot... and by that she means the captain... that I need to do something with my clothes. Max said a suit is a suit, and he didn't even care, 'cause he can't see it anyway, but Mrs Whitaker was very definite that I am not dressed appropriately. But this is the only suit I have... which my uncle gave me when I went for my interview. For so long I haven't worn anything apart from army garb. So, to be honest, I have no idea how to fix this. I wouldn't even know where to find a tailor."

Ellie chuckled. "This is about your wardrobe?"

"You are right. It is silly."

"I didn't say it was silly. But I am not sure I am the right person to help with this, because I am exactly in the same position. I haven't worn anything apart from a nurse's uniform for years it seems. But don't despair... I know someone who can help: Mim. Because of your persistent message delivery, Mim is going out with your Mr Whitaker now. She is exactly the right person to have an idea of what comprises appropriate attire to be seen with the Whitakers."

"Miss Hillman? That Mim? Oh, I don't think that is a good idea. She doesn't like me."

"She didn't like that you were doing your job. That is different."

"Pretty sure she cannot see the distinction."

* * *

They organised to meet with Mim after her shift. They sat waiting for her on the bench in the garden. She was in her uniform when she walked up. "So, what's this about?" she asked, eyeing Philip carefully. She was still suspicious of the 'Pinstripe-suit guy' who harassed her into to meeting with Max after the New Year's Dance. When she did eventually go and talk with Max Whitaker, it worked out for the best, reconnecting again after being separated by the war. Even so, she still found the pinstripe-suit fellow odd and awkward.

Mim noticed that he clung to Ellie's hand like a life raft. Ellie glanced his way. "Philip would like some advice," she said as a gentle prompt.

Mim waited expectantly. Philip squirmed and said nothing. Ellie cleared her throat and leaned over and whispered in his ear. He nodded. She spoke again. "Mim, sit down. Please."

Mim sat beside Ellie.

Ellie looked thoughtful, trying to speak to the situation without making it sound trivial. "Philip wants me to explain this to you. Mrs Whitaker has diagnosed Philip's attire to be inappropriate as her son's Personal Assistant. We thought you might help us update his wardrobe."

Mim laughed outright. "Me? I don't know anything about clothes, and especially men's wear. The only man I have ever helped dress is my father... and he wears gardening overalls: uncomplicated and unhindered by fashion trends."

"But you are engaged to a Whitaker now... you mix in their circle."

"The advantage of this arrangement primarily being that my fiancé is blind... and he doesn't care what I wear. Which I would have thought, also applies to his assistant."

"Mr Whitaker said that exactly!" Philip blurted out, quite passionately. "But his mother is insistent. I really want her off my back, so I have to do something."

Mim raised her brow. Mr Sinclair might not just be the embodiment of the whimpering ill-fitting suit that she took him for. Perhaps she had made that age old error of judging an assistant by his clothes. Even Max had urged her not to judge a book by its cover. She chuckled. "Well, *that* I do understand. You might remember I was harassed into meeting with Max and went along with it just to get someone off my back." She laughed. "I'm sorry Philip. I was pretty stressed, and I know I gave you a hard time. But I appreciate your dilemma... and I do happen to know someone who can help."

"You do?" Ellie said hopefully. "See Flip, I told you she would know how to go about this."

"Max's sister, Anna. She the perfect person to help: she has impeccable taste in fashion, and she *is* a Whitaker. You may not know this... but I used to be her governess. Ancient history I know, but I'm sure if I asked her, she would be willing to help."

Flip curiously looked at Ellie, as he felt her body go tense beside him. Her voice was strained. "Don't you think that is jumping from the frying-pan into the fire? Annabelle Whitaker is tarred with her mother's brush when it comes to arrogant and rude."

"Anna? She is a bit forthright for sure, but..."

Ellie cut her off. "I grew up in this neighbourhood, so I know exactly how she is."

"Yes, you are right. You did, of course; the community choir. But that was a long time ago. She has grown up and she is no longer that kid."

"Well, I believe the saying is that a leopard doesn't change its spots."

"Well, I guess ultimately it is up to you Philip. I do know Anna helped me dress for a date with the heir elect of the Grandfield dynasty. She is very good at it. See, I have the ring to prove it."

Ellie frowned and shook her head as she stared at the ring on her hand. "Don't you remember that you have both just noted that Max is blind."

"Well, I know my fiancé. And he sees more than his eyes allow." After all, Max defended Philip's work right from the start, even for someone who was stammering and shy. Mim acknowledged now, awkward or not, Philip made the practical difference between Max being able to engage in his life and being forced to stay out on the fringes. Philip Sinclair was always going to be part of her life with Max Whitaker. Mim knew what it was like to feel out of place because of clothes. Besides, if she helped Philip feel more comfortable, he might lose the pinstripe. That would be a bonus. That suit... well, it symbolised awkward. "I tell you what. Let me organise with Anna to meet you and then you can decide from there."

* * *

Flip hardly could believe that Anna Whitaker would be an ally. It sounded too close to equality, and equality was something that Flip was not used to. Anna was his boss's sister. Did the name of Whitaker technically make her his boss as well? Flip also worked with Anna's fiancé, Richard Barnes. Rick was Tibby's son and had been appointed as the hospital accountant, and their first major project together had been to organise the submissions for the lawyers to transfer the administration of the hospital to the Whitaker Foundation. It was hectic and busy and insanely pressured by an urgency from Max to get this sorted. Normally these things were delayed by red tape, legal and political protocols. But it seemed that there was a postwar amnesty of favour over efforts that would rehabilitate and rebuild a wounded society. Max jumped on that with both legs... all be it that one of those legs was an artificial one. It was the way the world was now. Adaption was the new call to arms.

Even though Flip wasn't convinced Anna would take him seriously, he took the leap and met with her in the Seamstress' room, where the sewing and mending for the hospital was attended to.

Anna shook his hand warmly. "Mim tells me I have to be very kind to you because Max needs you... which is something I already know, of course."

Flip stared at Miss Anna Whitaker. He often saw her flitting around the hospital, like some bright sunbird. Very different to the time she had been sitting on the bench in the garden in the evening shadows with her brother. She wasn't that different from how he remembered her during their choir days. She hadn't changed as much as Mim had insisted. Still fancy. Still smart. Still privileged.

"So, Mr Sinclair... what is your budget?"

"Budget?"

"For your wardrobe update..."

"Umm... I'm not sure. I cannot afford anything too expensive, but I... I was thinking that perhaps I could pay it off? I know this is important to your mother."

"My mother? What do *your* clothes have to do with *my* mother?"

He squirmed. "Your mother tells me that I am shaming Mr Whitaker by not having the right sort of wardrobe. I would never intend to..."

"How has she made this about Father? I can't imagine that you would have very much to do with him."

"No, not your father... *Captain* Whitaker... *Max Whitaker*. What I wear is apparently reflecting badly on my job as his Personal Assistant."

Anna closed her eyes and levelled her breathing. "Mr Sinclair... Philip... can I call you that?"

Ellie had asked him the same thing once. That was respectful. Even kind. Ellie might not have the full story about Anna Whitaker after all. He nodded.

"Philip, I did not meet with you because I thought you were shaming anyone. I thought it was so you could feel more comfortable. Max needs you. Regardless of what my mother says, you have been helping him so much already, and your clothes haven't hindered you any to this point. Perhaps you don't need a new suit after all."

Flip sighed. People kept saying that... except the formidable Mrs Whitaker. "Oh... but I would rather just do it. No disrespect Miss Anna, but your mother really does go on about it."

Flip jolted as Anna laughed... a bright tinkle that sprinkled relief over the seamstress' room. "Well Philip, I think you have summed up the situation sublimely. You know... I am familiar with how Mother thinks, and I believe the problem is not just the suit, it is about the lack of variety. So, let's fix this. Let me introduce to you Mrs Hargrave. She has been making and mending clothes and staff-uniforms at Grandfield since the beginning of time. She is very clever." It was not long before Mrs Hargrave came in from delivering some uniforms to the laundry for pressing.

Mrs Hargrave stood and stared with a frown at the suit Philip was wearing. Anna smiled in an attempt to reassure Philip that this was the right person to address his dilemma. Anna considered his suit. "I think the fabric is fine. Navy pinstripe is smart. Can you do anything to make it fit better... and lose some of that old-fashioned feel?"

Mrs Hargrave grunted as she gave it a perfunctory tug here and there. "The fabric is worn here, and here... it needs taking in here and here." She took a few measurements. "Right. Take it off." Philip didn't move. "Now!" she said efficiently.

Flip's eyes went wide. "Off? Here?"

"Yes. I can't sew it on you."

"But I didn't bring a change of clothes."

Anna shrugged. "Oh, don't worry. I have a couple of suits here for you to try."

Anna handed him a new shirt. The shirt from his uncle was too big; worn around the collar and cuffs as he washed it out every evening. He went behind the screen and eyed the three different suits hanging on a rack: a mid-grey; a light brown; and traditional black. Surely, he didn't have to choose between these. He put on the grey pants and jacket. Oh, they fitted so well... nothing like his hand-me-down pinstripe. He didn't actually know suits could be comfortable to wear. He stood a little straighter as he walked out behind the screen. Yes. He liked this one. Anna tilted her head as she held up a blue tie and then a maroon one against his shirt. She put a hat on his head and adjusted the brim. "Yes. This works. Very debonaire. Now try the taupe."

Flip frowned as he stood in front of a long mirror. Who calls brown, 'taupe'? Anna Whitaker evidently. He tried the 'taupe' suit and was immediately uncertain. This was even more comfortable. Colour didn't matter to him. "Okay, I like this one better... it feels good." Really good. He had no idea how expensive these suits would be.

"Excellent!" said Anna as she tried a few different ties to add to the blue and maroon. "Let me give you a lesson in suits. Using a different tie creates a whole new outfit with the same suit. See how these go with the grey as well. You can even wear grey pants and the taupe jacket and so on. Creates more options."

Flip raised his brow. It really didn't make that much difference to him. Just having one suit that fits well would meet the brief.

Anna made sure that Mrs Hargrave checked the fit and then instructed him to try the black.

Flip hedged. "Oh, this is a very formal suit. It looks highbrow for me. I don't think I will be needing this."

"Well, just try it on."

He complied. He rolled his shoulders. So different from army issue. She tied the bow tie and tilted the mirror. "Don't you think that looks very suave? Ellie will sing brighter with you by her side in this."

Flip jolted. "Ellie?"

"Oh come. Everyone knows you hold a torch for her. I suggest that you don't dress for Max – he is as blind as a bat. But Ellie... Ellie has her eyes wide open. You do look very handsome in this, Mr Sinclair."

Flip lowered his voice. "Does everyone know this?"

"Know what? That you look good in a bow tie? I think the suit speaks for itself."

"No... I mean, about Ellie..."

Anna shrugged. "Pretty sure..."

He looked a little panicked. "Does Ellie know?"

"Well, of that I am not sure. Have you ever told her?"

"Me? Of course not."

"Well, why not?"

"Because she is Ellie Pollard..." He said that as if it explained everything.

"And you are Philip Sinclair." She straightened his tie again and positioned him in front of the mirror again. "I can't speak to your relationship with Ellie, but I can help with the wardrobe. I'm a great believer in the principle that if we know our clothes work, the flow on is greater confidence. You asked for my help? Okay... here is my solution. I will get three shirts that fit you properly for a change of colour; five ties offer even more options. If we combine these with the pinstripe and these other suits, remembering that you can mix pants and jackets, you should..."

Flips eyes grew wide, and his frown deepened. "That's ridiculous!"

"No, it's not. Mix-and-match is not just a woman's fashion strategy. Lots of men do it too."

"What I mean is... with what you have suggested I have calculated I will have one hundred and thirty-five different combinations of office wear."

"Really? One hundred and thirty-five! How about that? I had no idea it would be so many. Max said you were good at what you did. To calculate that so quickly – that's impressive! But honestly it simply means that any choice of shirt, tie, jacket, or pants will look very smart, so you don't have to worry about what goes with what. Just trust me – it does. If you rotate wearing them evenly, they will hardly wear out. You literally have a wardrobe here that will last forever. And what is best, is that Mother need never worry about you looking boring or worn out ever again."

Philip looked at the black suit he was wearing in the mirror. "Surely, I don't need this as well!"

Anna was very matter of fact. "Oh, absolutely you need a dinner suit. There will be very special occasions, like the Gala, or concerts and all sorts of official events, where you will be required to accompany my brother, so you might as well look the part. Black suit is a must. Don't you think it looks very smart?"

"I think this is all very expensive, and way over the top."

Anna smiled. "I know it does seem like a lot... but I also know my mother. Trust me. This will get her off your back. This is the way I see this working: you pay for the alterations to your navy pinstripe, one shirt and one tie. I have organised with Max to pay for the rest, out of your unpaid overtime as a once off legitimate bonus package. You always put in much more than is ever recognised, and you do everything asked of you without even a pause. You are a good man Philip Sinclair, and I sincerely don't have a habit of saying things like that unless I believe them to be true in the most genuine way. I am so grateful that Max found you... or, as it might be, you found him."

* * *

15

Ellie walked past Flip's desk. She often found a way to detour down that corridor when she was doing rounds. She smiled and paused. "I'm guessing your visit with the seamstress was successful. You look very smart in your suit today, Mr Sinclair." She wasn't going to give Anna any credit for this. "The grey suits you!" she said with a grin. Pun intended. She smiled because shy awkward Flip Sinclair was now professional handsome Flip Sinclair.

He blinked. "Do you think it's okay? Not too much?"

"Not too much for me. That other suit... the way it was... if I am honest, it didn't really fit that well. But this... Flip, this makes you look so professional. Mrs Whitaker has no cause to complain ever again."

"Really? Why didn't you say something before?"

"You know, I don't really think it matters what you wear. Besides, I thought it would distress you. And it is kinda my job to check you're okay. What could you have done about it anyway?"

He frowned. "Well, I could have done this." He rubbed his brow as a whole lot of thoughts exploded through his mind like shrapnel. "Excuse me Ellie, but I have a fair bit of work to do just now. I'll catch up with you after work." For the first time in his life,

Flip turned away from Ellie, to address the list of things that sat on his schedule for the morning.

Ellie was standing right there, but suddenly she was no longer the centre of Flip's stammering, faltering universe. Whenever she popped by, he always stopped what he was doing and awkwardly tried to make small talk. Not that he was good at it, but she appreciated that he tried, and she could help put him at ease and make him smile. Ellie stood there uncertain. Flip continued on with his work. Eventually she nodded. "Good day Mr Sinclair," she said as she turned and left.

"Bye Ellie. I'll see you this afternoon after your shift." Flip was being fair dinkum. He did have a lot of things to attend to. But as she walked away, he put down his pen and rubbed his brow again. Something occurred to him as Ellie stood there just now. Ellie saw him as part of her 'job'; always making sure he was okay, even when he wasn't her patient. Sure, Ellie was looking out for him, but it felt like the way she had looked after her little brothers when she was younger. Ellie had been forced into being a parent way before her time because her mum fought too many demons, and her stepfather breezed in and out of their lives with no consistency or substance. Just dandelion fluff. Perhaps that's why nursing came so natural to Ellie: always the big sister; always the carer. Becoming a nurse was not a big leap for her. When Ellie declared they were friends forever, he had hoped it was as equals needing each other throughout all seasons of their lives, but perhaps it was just her inner carer kicking in.

The episode of the suit-fittings was confusing for Flip. Mrs Whitaker believed that clothes were extremely important, yet she had very little interest in character. His mum always said that clothes didn't matter as much as character did. Of course, he allowed that his mother used it to justify a very tight budget, but it was wisdom that endured. What he found confusing was that he *felt* different in these new clothes. He felt his confidence rise, just like Anna suggested. Even though these clothes made him look like everyone else on the outside, an internal confidence had settled over him as he tied his new tie and buttoned his new jacket.

Yes, he did have something to offer. Anna had sincerely encouraged him as a 'good man'. The captain certainly saw worth in his work. As time went on, Flip was able to really believe what Max said – that he was not just rescuing Flip again, dragging him from another life-and-death disaster. Max Whitaker really valued what he had to contribute. Flip knew his work was solid, but now he realised he had something else... something important. He had something that Doctor Redmond did not have; something Billy did not have. He had integrity and character. He wasn't going to lead Ellie on for distraction or amusement while he had another fiancé hanging in the wings. He wasn't going to bully her into doing what he required whether she wanted to be with him or not. Suddenly Flip felt the possibility that Ellie could actually like him, for himself. It was a truth that settled down into his heart, like a seed nestling in freshly turned soil. Ellie said she admired his sort of strong. As eligible suitors go, he legitimately could be the next strong, composed, capable person in her life, not just for a short reprise, but for the whole song. A song that went on for their entire lives.

Each time they went walking, it could be for real and not just waiting for someone else to push him aside to come in and take his place. But Flip also had another significant realisation. This would only be possible if Ellie saw him differently... more than a childhood victim, more than a washed-up solider, more than the clean-cut suit he wore now. And most of all, it could only be if she wasn't relegating him to being another one of her kid brothers who became her 'job' to take care of.

* * *

Ellie walked away from Flip's desk in a daze. She had been so pleased that Flip was finding his place. He stuttered less; awkward pauses interrupted the flow of their conversations less. But she had rarely witnessed him being that assertive with anyone, much less with her. Flip said he would meet her after her shift ended, just as they usually did, but she frowned as she walked down the corridor. Something had changed. He had been so upset by what she said about his clothes. That was exactly what she was trying to forestall. Well, at least she was right about one thing. He did look very handsome. She always thought Flip was goodlooking. Perhaps that was why Billy had been so jealous of him. Even so, Flip's shyness somehow neutralised any benefit that would normally offer. What if she had drawn him out of his shell, just to have him turn away and be this great, fantastic confident person for someone else? Apparently, he really did only think of her as a friend. End of story. Was it possible, that, just by being fitted for a suit, some of that Anna Whitaker Grandfield arrogance had rubbed off on him. Mim had been so confident that Anna had really grown up into a mature and considerate woman but endorsing that appointment with Anna and the seamstress may have been Ellie's biggest mistake.

Just then, Anna walked through the corridor towards her with her bubbly smile. Ellie frowned. Anna was another Billy the Bully. Just because she was pretty with a winning smile, it didn't make it less so. Ellie was so over bullies! She was over the way they kept messing up her life and her plans, and she was over the fact that she never stood up to them.

"Good morning, Ellie," Anna was saying brightly. It was like Ellie could hear her voice but was unable to distinguish the words she was speaking. "I am just on my way to see Max. I'm assuming he's in since you're coming from that direction." Anna was always buoyant. It was like it was impossible for her to sink. "What did you think about Philip's new wardrobe? Did we do okay?" The way she said it, Ellie knew Anna had no doubt that she believed they had actually knocked the brief right out of the park. A cricket metaphor: a six, hit way over the boundary line.

Ellie's frown deepened. "Do you want to know what I think? I think you have a hide to always be poking your stuck-up nose into what is not your business! Let Philip alone and leave me alone. Just because you have a seat on the Board of this Hospital, it doesn't give you a free pass into everyone's life!" Ellie stormed off down the corridor.

Anna stared after her. Every past put-down thrown at Anna by someone in a nursing uniform swung around and slapped her hard across the face like a cold fish. She shook her head stunned, blinked hard, and then ran after her. "Ellie? Ellie!"

Ellie stopped and stared at her. "What? I am sure you have quite done enough!"

"I only helped Philip because Mim asked me too. Why do you think I would get involved where I was not asked?"

"Oh please! I'm surprised you even got involved since you are so far above us. We are not good enough for you and your snobby Grandfield types!"

"But you just said..."

"Forget it, Miss Whitaker! Forget it. Everywhere you go you just cause me trouble! I think that I am pretty right to avoid you. I don't need the aggravation or the trouble! I'm over it! Good day, Miss

Whitaker. I will not detain you further from your duties. You will find Mr Whitaker in his office."

"Ellie, I can see you are angry, and I suspect this is not just about Philip's suits. Can't we sort this out? Please! I need to know what's happened. Is it nursing school, or something I said as a kid? I sincerely don't understand. I know that growing up in my Grandfield bubble did not equip me well to deal with life outside. Please, can I buy you a coffee and lunch on your break? We have to work together now. Please... help me understand."

Ellie tried to resist Anna's plea. She didn't want to be sucked into her charming vortex like everyone else. But she relented. Perhaps giving her some insight into how she really was, might shake her tree a little. After all, she was right about that. They were going to keep bumping into each other. There were not that many corridors in this house.

The last thing Ellie wanted was to be seen with Anna Whitaker in the dining room, so she organised to meet in the small teahouse near the council gardens a couple of blocks away. While Ellie sat and waited for Anna in the undercover outdoor area, she eyed a little butcher bird, perched on the back of a chair at the next table.

A butcher bird. Ellie thought about the little butcher bird who sang his heart out on the roof-top when she decided to apply to nursing school. She thought about those grand ideas he inspired about singing her own song. Did it matter if other people liked her own song or not? Ellie always had approval as she sang for the soldiers, but what about the song of her soul? Why did it matter to her so much that Anna never thought she was good enough to be her equal? Mostly Ellie did remember to sing. But sometimes the music of her heart just seemed to clash and crash... a discordant sound in her ears.

It was moments like this morning, when Flip turned away, that it felt like there was this internal spinning cog that could never spin fast enough to make everything work in time, synchronising who she was with her higher purpose.

Anna arrived and sat down. She frowned as she looked through the door to the shadows inside the cafe. "Last time I was here, I thought I was going to die. I could hardly move. I was so depleted and dry. It was not that long ago... and yet here I am in a totally different place. Marlie and Tibby have literally saved my life. They are heroes of my story, and no one will never know, because they refuse to publish their care." Anna cleared her throat and shook her head as if clearing the fog. "I'm sorry... being here brought that back. Can I order something for you?"

They ordered their tea. And a sandwich each. Simple and unpretentious. Ellie noted that.

Anna didn't really know where to start. "Ellie, is this about Nursing School? I know you avoided me because Sister Perry had it in for me. But then you were always the better nurse. I'm sure you know that."

Ellie blinked. She was taken off guard because Anna so quickly conceded that. "So, you're not mad because I kept my distance back then?"

"I had hoped for a friend. I was desperately lonely. I thought I knew what I was getting into when applied to do the Nursing course. But it was nothing at all how I pictured it in my head. Nursing was cruel to me, and I felt trapped. But it was not just the job. How I didn't get a full-blown septicaemia the way the skin on my hands kept breaking down, is beyond me. Thing is... people constantly told me I was weak because I was used to privilege, and I should pull myself together. But it was more than that. That was my Western Front. I limped back here wounded like the patients admitted here. I was quite sincere when I said Tibby and Marlie saved my life."

Ellie studied her sandwich. She had not expected to feel sympathy for Anna. She took a bite and steadied her resolve to be firm in making her point.

Anna took a sip of her tea. "You know... you said that I was in the community choir with you. But to be really honest, I don't remember too much about that. Miss Lambert took most of my singing lessons at home."

"So, you don't remember snubbing me?"

"I'm sorry... I really don't. I only remember you singing so beautifully... being singing royalty. Perhaps I was embarrassed."

Ellie scoffed. Anna Whitaker embarrassed? Hardly. "Miss Lambert lined me up to be your 'special friend'. But you would have nothing to do with me. You even wouldn't let me wait with you until Tibby came to pick you up... you couldn't walk home fast enough to get away from me."

Anna stared at her. Suddenly she was back on the street... walking home, being swooped by a magpie that had moments before been singing so beautifully. She remembered feeling that the choir was the same... sings beautifully but is actually dangerous. The choir had been used by her mother to keep her away from Chrissy. More than that, Chrissy was so sick at that moment she was dying, and Anna wasn't there beside her.

Anna stared at Ellie and went a shade paler.

Ellie nodded as she saw a look of revelation dawn in Anna's eyes. She watched her swallow. "You remember now, don't you?" Ellie felt kind of vindicated that she wasn't just making this up. This was history. Her history.

Anna said nothing for a long time. She didn't expect Ellie to understand any more now than she did back then. But she thought it was reasonable that she at least knew a little of what had happened. "I can see how you would have thought me aloof and disinterested. What you don't know, is that my mother discouraged me from being part of the choir right from the start, and she insisted my lessons only be conducted at home. Miss Lambert told me the choir would be a great way to learn blending harmonies with others. I remember begging Mother to allow me to join, and I went a couple of times, but I guess I felt so out of water it was hard to think I could ever really be a part of it. The only day that Mother really insisted that I go to the community hall for practice was that day, the day I walked home. It was also the day that my best friend, my heart sister, my kindred spirit... Tibby's daughter Chrissy was..." Anna swallowed hard and blinked quickly from the steam rising from her teacup as she took a sip. "Chrissy was at that moment knocking on heaven's door and saying goodbye without me. It took me a long time to forgive my mother for that, or even to feel I wanted to participate in anything much again. Rick suggested that perhaps I went nursing as penance for not being there to care for her. Perhaps he was right. I'm sorry I wasn't more attentive to you Ellie that day. I feel sad in a way... because I suspect that under different circumstances, we might have been great friends."

Unprompted tears stung Ellie's eyes, and she swallowed hard. All this time she had held Anna to account for snobbish elitism when she was just a kid dealing with a broken heart and grief too deep to describe. Just like her. She had her childhood robbed as well. Ellie swallowed again and she reached out and touched her hand. "Anna

I am so sorry. Not just that you missed out on the choir, but that your friend was taken from you."

"Thank you, Ellie. I am too."

"Tibby came and offered me some paid work in the kitchen with Marlie. It was just after my little sister died. I felt so sad. It helped me to know that someone really understood what it meant to have lost someone too. I never thought that someone could be you as well. That job was like a lifeline... my mother really wasn't the same after our little Myrtle got her angel wings. That's what we called the day she left... her Wing-day. Some people at church were upset with us because they said that angels are God's special creatures, and people don't turn into angels when they die. I know that of course, but it just helps to think that she is in heaven, healthy and strong, without the pain her little life was filled with. It was easier to say it that way for my brothers and sister too."

Anna looked into her empty cup and refilled it from the teapot. Every time she poured a cup it reminded her of Chrissy. It was something that never went away. "I like that. Wing-day. Chrissy had her Wing-day too. I don't think God would judge us because we find comfort in some theological fuzziness. What is important is that they are together. Chrissy was good with little ones, so perhaps her and Myrtle are laughing and playing together right now. I need to apologise Ellie, on another account. I was so angry that Tibby hired another girl. I thought he was just replacing Chrissy too quickly. I never considered how impossibly hard that must have been on both Tibby and Marlie. They were being the heroes in your life too. I can see that now."

Ellie swallowed again. She was embarrassed to realise she had her own personal brand of snobbery. "Anna? I'm sorry I judged you so harshly. I'm sorry I didn't listen to more than just the words that you spoke. I wonder if you would consider singing with me sometime. We could explore some of those harmonies we used to do in choir that you missed out on. I still have lessons with Miss Lambert. She could help us."

The sadness in Anna's eyes softened and she smiled. "I would really like that, Ellie. I would. We could sing a song for Chrissy and Myrtle."

* * *

Ellie sat on a bench outside the Glasshouse and looked again at the watch that was pinned to the bib of her nurses' apron. It had been a big day and her conversation with Anna had just piled in more things that she needed to think about. One thing she didn't want to think about, was that Flip was moving on without her. But as the minutes slowly ticked on, she had to concede that this was most probably what had happened. She sighed and stood up to abandon her post. As she turned, Philip walked up with his hands behind his back. He looked so handsome in his grey suit, his face thoughtful.

"My apologies Ellie. I came straight from the office. Mr Whitaker had some meetings that ran over."

"I thought after this morning that you might not want to go walking anymore. You seemed quite angry with me."

"I said I would meet you after work. I am a man of my word Ellie."

"I know. I know. I just don't understand. I didn't think that what I said was all that offensive. I was trying to compliment you on your new suit. I thought... I still do... I think you look good."

"Well, thank you. I appreciate that. Actually, you didn't really say anything wrong at all. I really did have a lot of things to do today. I was genuinely busy. Mr Whitaker had a full day. I wasn't just giving you the brush off." He stood there... familiar strains of awkward.

Ellie stood to her feet. "It's okay Flip. Everyone seems busy nowadays..."

"But I did have something I wanted to talk to you about. It is more of an awareness on my part, but this morning was not the time to go into it, so thank you for waiting." He cleared his throat and softened his tone. "I did realise how it seemed, so I wanted to give you these." He pulled a bouquet of flowers from behind his back and pressed the simple flowers into her hand. "I'm sorry I was short with you. You are so special Ellie Pollard... more than any other girl I know."

He watched a range of emotions flash through Ellie's eyes as she stared at the bouquet of flowers in her hands. She had said to Flip once, that he was good at delivering messages. Well, she considered this was the most important message he had ever delivered. Someone had finally given her flowers, not for singing a song, or because someone had died. Just for her being her.

"Ellie, I know that you have said that we are friends forever. I know that is true. But something else is true. I am in love with my best friend... and I cannot pretend it is otherwise anymore. I want to keep company with you, not because it is in some way protecting you from unwanted suitors, but because I want to be that suitor myself."

Ellie stared at him, her eyes wide behind the lenses of her glasses. Had they both been silently holding this same fear from each other?

Flip swallowed and kept going. "And I suppose I wanted to clarify that. I don't want to be your patient, or your job, or a chore, or someone you feel obligated to care for. I want to be the one who does life with you, in all of its tasks and duties and joys, because I love you. You don't have to answer straight away of course, as I do suppose this is different to how you have seen me, but I really want you to consider what I have said. You can let me know whether this is something that you are open to." For once, Flip didn't apologise, or qualify, or dismiss, or minimise. He just waited. He stood there, his heart beating loudly in his chest, and when Ellie didn't respond, he quietly stepped back. "I'll call on you tomorrow, Ellie. And you should know that I will keep coming until you tell me that you have no feelings for me, or that you want me to stop." He turned to go.

"Flip, wait! There is no point having you come back tomorrow, because I have no doubt that you would keep coming indefinitely. I've seen you do it. You have proven you can be rather relentless. You have that sort of tenacity..." His own version of strong.

Flip's face sank. Would she so quickly squash this brave signal from his heart? It was easier to lift a flag under enemy fire. But he would not be a Billy and crush her into being his girlfriend if her heart was somewhere else. This was her choice too. He nodded, resigned. "I see..." He turned to go.

"Flip! Where are you going? What I mean is that you don't have to deliver your message again and again, because I have an answer for you right now."

"Oh. Well, thank you for hearing me out Ellie..."

"Please... I need you to listen to my answer too!"

"Okay. Say your piece...". Flip didn't want to hear the *'you're a nice guy and a good friend, but...'* speech. He stared at the ground.

"Flip, you are so different from the others in my life, and that has always caught my attention. It seemed that everything was pulling us apart so it could never be us. Just us. I had to step back when we were kids because I was so worried that Billy would hurt you again. Then the war started and went on and on... and then the same thing happened to Arthur right here, where we were supposed to be in a safe place. And yet Flip, you have always been the person who keeps coming back, you keep showing up with your beautiful messages. I didn't have men who did that in my life growing up. But you are different. You have never given up on me. I know I am used to being a big sister, and even a nursing sister... but I don't think of you as a job or a chore. It is just that the idea of being someone's girlfriend just because I want to, and not because I am afraid... this is new to me." Ellie studied the flowers in the bouquet. Every bloom fragile and perfect. "I find your invitation different because this time no one is forcing me; or I am not being charmed into believing a version of a relationship which is not real. I realise I don't know how to do this very well yet, and I do fall back into sistering because that is pretty much all I have ever known. But I do know that I trust you... and I do know that we can learn how to do this together." She smiled as she took a deep breath of the fragrance of the flowers in her arms. "I think I understand how you feel, because I also have been in love with my best friend for a while now, and if I was telling secrets I would say I have had a crush on him since we were singing together in the choir as kids."

Flip raised his eyes and gazed full into her face. He shook his head in amazement. "You are so full of surprises Ellie Pollard. I hardly know what to think. *You* had a crush on *me*?"

"I think you are the best, Flip Sinclair... I liked standing next to you in choir, and I am relieved that I don't have to worry that I might cause you danger, or scare you away, any longer."

Someone from the kitchen came running up the path. "Sister Pollard! Everyone is wondering if you are coming to sing tonight. The patients are waiting to start their meal," she said breathlessly.

"Oh goodness... is that the time already? Actually, tell them to start eating... and let them know that I will sing at the end of the meal today." The tread of the messenger's feet faded as she ran back down the path. Ellie reached out her hand. "Now I have a question for you Flip Sinclair. Will you sing a duet with me tonight?"

"In front of everyone?"

"No... just you and me. If it just so happens that there are others who are lucky enough to eavesdrop on our song, then so be it."

"Oh Ellie... it would be my privilege to sing with you. I want to accompany, harmonize, and blend our songs until my very last breath. That is my promise."

"That is a promise I give to you as well." Ellie twisted her hand in his, making that seal of a friendship in their unique shake. Then she pulled his hand forward and kissed him on the cheek. He gathered her in his arms and kissed her, their lips melting together.

"I have wanted to do that for the longest time," he whispered.

Eventually she tugged his hand. "Come, we have a duet to sing that will make the birds in this garden unable to resist joining in.

They will bear witness to the music which has brought us together...
a song that is sweet and strong. Perhaps it can soothe the bitterness
from even a Great War."

They walked towards the dining room, arm in arm, and
synchronised with their steps they both let out a breath. "Hmm–
Hmm–Ahhh!". A duet was waiting to be sung. The harmony of their
hearts blended and merged, and it felt like this song had been waiting
for such a long time to be heard. It felt like destiny.

⌘ ⌘ ⌘

The End

Other books by this author

Matt's Boys of Wattle Creek

Maggie & Minotaur

Rose's Diary

Gems of Australia Series:
Sapphires of Hope
Rubies of Ambition
Emerald Dreams

Homes of Healing Series:
The Beachside Cottage
Petra Downs
The Writer's Retreat

Guthrie's Lot Series:
A Spacious Place
A Level Path
The Crying Tree

Pioneers of Grace Series:
Time of Grace
Circle of Grace
Journey of Grace
Mask of Grace
Crucible of Grace
Sculpture of Grace

Bottlebrush Grove Series

Shadows in the Corners
The Ragged Edges
Scratches across the Surface
Cracks through the Core

Children's Book

The Bush Olympics.
The Great Fly Hunter

Non-Fiction

Reflections in the Bible – Daniel

Reflections in the Bible – Abraham

Reflections in the Bible – Elijah

Reflections in the Bible – Job

Reflections in the Bible – David

Reflections in the Bible – Elisha

Reflections in the Bible – Joseph

Reflections in the Bible – Kings of Judah

Reflections in the Bible – Nehemiah

Reflections in the Bible – Samuel